Josie's Journey:
Trail of Change

By

Mindy Lou Johnston

Josie's Journey: Trail of Change

Thank you to my husband and his never-ending encouragement. Thank you to the boys of Roscommon County Juvenile Detention (2019) for loving Josie; it fueled me to follow through with the book. Thank you to everyone who always knew I was full of creative mischief and encouraged it.

Be happy---Mindy Lou

Josie's Journey: Trail of Change

<u>CHAPTERS</u>

CHAPTER ONE: BREATHE

The yellow and orange leaves were rustling musically in the cool breeze. The majority of the fall leaves have already fallen, leaving the stark, dark fingers of the tree's branches reaching up from frozen the soil. The sun had been up long enough to melt the heavy frost that had clung delicately to every surface this morning. Josie took a deep breath, smelling the river's moisture mingled with the farm yard's earthy fragrance. She needed to focus on all the things that were real in the world; that is why she concentrated on that aroma…or else she would cry. "I am too old to be crying." Even though she told herself these things aloud, the tears were in her eyes. "I will be thirteen in two days. Much too old to cry. Crying doesn't solve anything. The farm chores still need to be done." Taking a deep breath, she reminded herself no matter what: *"the cows need milked, the stock need fed, and life goes on."*

She walked to the well cranking the wind last drawing up a bucket of water to fill the trough. She did this several times a day so she would never need to add more than one bucket at a time to keep the trough full. These simple motions of filling the trough or feeding the stock were so ingrained in her movements that she didn't think, only acted. Josie deliberately forced herself to focus on the task at hand on this crisp fall morning, not spilling a drop of water from the bucket while negotiating the slight slope to the trough. "The water is real…the bucket is real," Josie said over and over again in her mind. Putting down the bucket after emptying it to the trough, she led the livestock out to the pasture for the day in some trance-like state.

On November 3rd, not too many more nice days before the pasture would be blanketed in thick snow, Josie thought then, went into the spacious, meticulously cleaned barn to feed the flock of chickens and collect their eggs. She almost tripped over the bucket of milk from earlier that morning, "Good thing the morning was cool," Josie thought, chiding herself for being forgetful while carrying the milk to the spring house. "How could I be so irresponsible?" Josie told herself about the potential of the milk turning sour or a cow kicking

over the bucket. Josie momentarily forgot what hardship waited for her inside the house in her moment of self-recusal. "Oh, the eggs…I needed to collect the eggs. I am so scattered this morning," she reminded herself mid-stride. Then, she hastened away from the house.

Josie could hear the distinct sound of digging from the hillside above the house even though she was in the barn. The sound of the frozen ground coarsely scraping at the metal of the shovel made her heart race and her sick to her stomach. "Isn't there anything else that needed to be done out here?" she questioned herself aloud while looking around in wide-eyed desperation. Josie hastily grabbed a rake and began vigorously cleaning the stalls, the stalls that were already clean. She had cleaned them last night, twice. Yet, she continued to furiously rake the stalls with some buried primal drive to drown out the sound of the digging. Exhausted, breathing hard, Josie collapsed into a frail mass on the hay pile, still not crying. She knew she couldn't hide in the barn all morning, no matter how much she wanted to. More sooner than later, she would have to take the eggs in the house and face life, her new life

Staring down at her well-worn moccasins, trying to gain courage, Josie willed her begrudging feet to carry her into the house. This was the first time she could remember ever dreading going inside her home, knowing that she came one more step closer to an unknown life with each step towards the house. While walking, she focused on the cream-colored yarn from her sock sticking out from a hole where her big toe was on her left moccasin. Josie had darned that sock with red thread because it was pretty. Her mother told her, "It is better to not draw attention to things that are not supposed to exist." It was her Ma's way of correcting her thread choice. A slight smile moved across her face with the memory. Somewhere lost in her memories while walking to the house from the barn, the nerve grating digging had stopped echoing down from the hillside, gratefully, maybe her heart and stomach would calm. Josie stepped up to the back door pausing long enough to take a deep breath, smoothed her dress, and hair in the hope of looking presentable. She slipped silently in the backdoor, shutting it just as silently behind her. Josie set the eggs on the table, trying to be invisible. Her mouth was dry, and her palms were sweaty enough to be mistaken for the Mississippi.

She wanted to run, but where? Instead, she stood frozen in her aunt's icy glare.

"Where have you been, Josephine?" her frosty blue eyes were assessing Josie's home-spun appearance with disdain.

Apologetically Josie said while looking at the ground, "I had to do the morning chores, Aunt Susan."

"Your chores couldn't wait, Josephine? Your uncle and I are busy people; yet, we came all this way to help…and you disappear to do chores. Don't you have 'hired' help to do the chores? If I didn't love my brother so very much, I wouldn't even be here in this backward, socially unfit place. Do you understand me, Josephine?"

Aunt Susan was dressed in the latest style with pale hands on her hips. Josie studied the delicate nature of Aunt Susan's hands, doubting that she had ever done any chores in her life. The only thing Josie had ever seen Aunt Susan do that could even remotely be construed as a chore was pour tea. Aunt Susan was pouring tea at some stuffy event that Pa made her go to at Aunt Susan's high-fluting house in Quincy after the Lincoln-Douglas debate a couple of years ago. She poured tea in a

fancy dress, so that couldn't count as a real chore. "Why couldn't her father be here now instead of his sister?" the thought darted across her mind like flushing a pheasant from the brush.

Josie knew that speaking or making eye contact would incur her aunt's wrath. Her tired mind could come up with the only solution was to nod her head in understanding while thinking how unlike her father and his sister were in temperament. She quietly prayed that facing Aunt Susan would be the worst of her day; unfortunately, this was going to be the easier part of the day, she knew what lay ahead of her still.

Josie heard Aunt Susan's husband, Uncle Tom, come in the door behind her. His presence was enough to make every hair on her body stand on end. The sound of him breathing made her clench her teeth in disgust. She absolutely loathed Uncle Tom. Worse yet, she hated that he was here now on this day of all days. However, it was her fault that her aunt and uncle were here on the farm now. Desperate to save her mother, Josie had sent a message up the river with their neighbor, Sam, that Ma was very ill and needed a doctor. Sam took the note to the bank her Uncle Tom owned for Josie.

Josie's desperation led her aunt and that scoundrel uncle to be there with her now.

Josie felt her uncle's hot breath on the back of her neck tried to block out the memory of why she hated him. Aunt Susan and Uncle Tom were speaking; yet, their voices became the background noise to the vivid recollection that her weary mind slipped into...

***

She and Ma were working in the garden enjoying the pleasant morning when Pa was downriver working a couple of summers ago. They were surprised to see Uncle Tom come up the path in his shiny black city buggy. At first, Ma thought something was wrong with Pa. When Ma said that to him, he just laughed and said, "Thought you could use some supplies since you don't get to town often, and I wanted to get out of town for a drive." He didn't realize we got most of our supplies by boat—however, Ma and her thought that was awful considerate...right nice of him. Ma invited him to stay for lunch.

Uncle Tom seemed extremely anxious during lunch. He kept looking around nervously and sweating a river on a cool day. After lunch, Uncle

Tom's tone completely changed; he went from social to Sam hill mean. Suddenly he yelled at her to "Get the Hell out of there, you half-breed brat!" Josie ran and hid under her bed. Soon she could hear dishes breaking then, her Ma screaming, she couldn't hide any longer. She wanted and needed to help her Ma. Josie came to the kitchen doorway to see Ma with her shirt ripped halfway off and her arm cut with blood seeping. Uncle Tom had a knife to Ma's throat. Mama's skirt was lifted, and Uncle Tom was behind her… he…was violating her. Josie's breath caught loudly, causing Uncle Tom to look up slowly. He locked eyes and just gave her a leering grin. She wet herself; she was so upset; Josie hadn't done that since she was a baby.

Ma and Josie talked about what happened after Uncle Tom had left them later that day. They were sitting on the dock drying after swimming in the river to clean themselves. Ma said to her, "We are women, and we are Indian. We are disposable to a lot of people. That is why you have to always be strong, deep within yourself, so that nothing can break your spirit. Today was terrible, but I am alive, and if he tries again… I will kill him." Ma shortly after this incident got one of those small pocket guns, a derringer, from one of the boatmen.

Josie's Journey: Trail of Change

She always carried it in a special pocket she sewed into all her dresses. Ma meant business when she got that gun. That gun was to kill any person that was a danger. People would never know she carried that little gun. It was so well concealed.

***

Uncle Tom stated sharply, "The grave is dug," abruptly rousting Josie out of her memory of long ago and back to the present.

"Good! Let's get this distasteful matter finished, then get back to town. I have a charity tea this afternoon at three. If we leave soon, I will be able to attend."

Uncle Tom went to Ma's bed, lifted her limp body up, and carried it up the hill where Josie's little sister was buried. Josie wouldn't let him have the satisfaction of seeing her mother one last time or of touching her mother the last time. She waited until her aunt and uncle were asleep then, she sewed the bed quilt around her Ma, protecting her. Josie did beautiful feathery stitch work, trying her best to mimic her Ma's fine talent. Now, she followed her cocoon of needlecraft being carried up the hill as the breeze blew down the golden and orange leaves.

Uncle Tom heaved her Ma unceremoniously in the freshly dug hole, without a word, a pause, prayer, or anything…and began filling in the grave. She turned her head away to blink back a tear when she saw Aunt Susan check her timepiece. Josie stood there in a mixed state of anger and sorrow, wanting these interlopers of her grief just to leave. Nothing about their presence had improved anything. Standing there watching as every shovel full of dirt was placed over her mother, all she could think was, "This is real. Mama is really gone." Josie walked down the hill in a fog of emotion too complicated to describe, still smelling the scent of fresh-turned frozen earth while a shower of golden leaves embraced her. It had seemed with every shovel of dirt her emotions became muddy, like the nearby churning Mississippi River.

Josie went into the kitchen in an emotional haze and put water in the well-used coffee pot with some fresh grounds. "Coffee will help; it always helps. I need a plan." Josie said aloud. Speaking to herself was somehow helping her hold things mentally together today. Both of her parents often talked to themselves. Now she was. Suddenly, hearing the slam of the kitchen door behind Josie was shaken to the attention that she was not alone yet. Josie still had to contend with her aunt and uncle. "What more could they say? Though they were in a rush to get back to town," sarcastically, the words tumbled out of her mouth. She was gratefully not heard; her parents would have been ashamed of her disrespect.

"Josephine, your uncle and I want you to come with us to Quincy to live. We think that with the proper clothes and manner, you could pass for a full white." This statement was said with the same frosty glare that was always given to her by her aunt. Josie knew what her aunt wanted was something to talk about in her charity circle to make her look important in society. This offer was not an action done out of love and compassion or for Josie's well-being. Aunt Susan never was short on words to let her know her shortcomings. No, this was not an offer out of love.

"Josie, what your aunt is trying to say, is you could go to school, have beautiful clothes, and we could help you find a successful husband in a few years. I would personally be by your side. You could look at me like a second father. What we want is in your best interest. You are a beautiful young girl," Uncle Tom said with a sly smile. Josie almost vomited, knowing exactly why Uncle Tom wanted

her to come live with them; it repulsed and sickened her at the same time that he would even suggest it.

"This is our Christian duty to take you in…you are my brother's daughter. You, of course, would be introduced to the cream of society and would be expected to speak, act, and dress accordingly. This transition would be arranged under my tutelage. The clothes you're wearing are not acceptable in society, nor is wearing your hair in braids at your age. It will be a month before we can introduce you to society. You have been exposed to too much sun. We shall have to see a chemist to lighten your skin." Aunt Susan rattled on believing her way to live was the only way to live. She finally pauses to take a breath.

"I have already sent a message to my mother's people about her passing first thing this morning. I will be going to them as soon as someone arrives to take me."

"What if your father returns from that forsaken territory?" Aunt Susan asked with a raised eyebrow and her nostril-flaring in disbelief that he would actually return.

"Pa will find a letter telling him where to find me with my mother's people."

"Well, this does solve everything, doesn't it, Thomas?" With those words, Aunt Susan, in a clucking huff, put on her gloves and cloak and strolled outside without so much as a farewell.

Josie didn't hear her uncle answer her aunt's rhetorical question. He went outside looking down-cast to hitch the buggy. Josie just sat there listening as their wagon was hitched up, and she could finally hear the horse hooves clomped into the distance before breathing a sigh of tenuous relief. Josie added a splash of cold water to the hot coffee in the pot to settle the grounds, poured herself a cup, and apologized profusely to God for lying to her aunt and uncle. But there was no way in tarnation she was ever, ever going with them to live. The idea was beyond nightmare-worthy.

CHAPTER TWO: HERITAGE

Josie truly wished that she could go to her Ma's people. Cradling her hot cup of coffee, she sat in her favorite chair, letting her mind wander. Pa and Ma had moved here when they were first married. Her Ma's parents were dead then. The only family member she had was her grandfather. His health was not well for a long time, and he died a few months after her parents were married. After his death, no ties were holding her home. Ma had distant relatives she spoke of sometimes, cousins and such. Ma would tell stories about growing up in the village and the games she and the other children played. She explained how some Sioux tribes were more nomadic, but the missionaries taught her tribe to be more settled. Ma's pa was a Scots man that traded during the good weather,

and during the bad weather, he was home. One day he went to barter then, never came back.

Josie's mother was half-Sioux and half-Scot. Ma had been educated by the missionaries and her father, Josie's grandfather. She was blessed to be very well-read. However, still growing up in a Sioux village, she had learned the traditional skills of her people. It was unusual to be well educated mixed blood, but being a female with her education added to her rarity. Ma was a woman to learn anything and everything quickly. An unusual skill that her mother learned to make from the missionaries was cheese. Ma said, "Those old French missionaries loved their cheese." To make cheese is a skill that takes patience. Ma looked at cheesemaking as an art. There were so many varieties that a person could make if they knowledge.

Pa would always tell the story with a grin on his face on how he won his bride. The young braves came courting from many different bands of the tribe, offering ponies for ma. These braves would be enchanted by her beauty, kindness, humility, and quick mind. When these braves offered ponies, they were the very best; yet, they were always turned away without a reason why. Then Pa came

along with two Jersey milk cows. The braves laughed that he would offer that in marriage. Pa must have understood her heart because she accepted his proposal immediately. Mama would always laugh when Pa would tell the story. The story is true as the blue sky; two Jersey milk cows are out in the barn.

Swallowing the last dregs of her coffee, Josie's mind returned to the current situation. She poured another cup of coffee then sat down with a piece of paper to analyze her position at the farm. She had seen her Ma make such lists. Now it was her turn to take stock. Josie knew she was well provisioned for the winter here by herself. Ma and her filled the root cellar with potatoes, onions, carrots, squash, cabbage…you name it. Plus, the attic has all the dried apples, berries, and jerky. She did well with hunting this year, so the smokehouse was packed. The spring house was full of cheese, butter, and milk, and there were the eggs. She and Ma traded the cheese, milk, butter, and eggs to a couple of boatmen who come to our dock for flour, sugar, coffee, and whatnot that would continue. They also took that in trade if they had extra fresh meat when the boatmen happened along. She needed to figure out what she should trade to prevent spoilage before she could use it. Trade it for things that keep or for money. She was going to need cash now that...well, that Ma was gone.

When the boatmen docked to trade, they would usually bring news of Pa if he was working on the river. The boatmen would also bring us newspapers then, sit and visit. A lot of time, they would stay for supper. Josie has known quite a few of these men since she was born. Gruff and rugged as they may be, they always treated Ma with respect and her like some cherished part of their family. They would often show up with a little treat for her like a bag of nuts or some rock candy. One of the men they traded with, Big Mike, gave her a brand-new Bowie knife last summer. He said, "Anyone that can hunt like you, Josie, needs a good knife that can finish the other half of the job." Mike even showed Josie how to throw it, demonstrating his amazing skill. She thought that was one of the finest tricks she had ever seen, so she practiced to be as good as him every day.

"Big Mike and the others will continue to stop, and she will continue to trade," Josie thought, sipping the still scalding coffee. She sat at the kitchen table, making a list of things that needed to be done, things to trade, and her additional daily chores. Looking at everything written down on paper made her realize that she could solve significant problems independently. Josie also noticed that life wasn't so daunting when it was written down. Writing down everything in her head was like collecting the eggs in the barn and putting them in a basket.

Her coffee had grown cold. She topped off her cup with some hot coffee. The first thing on Josie's list was she needed to strip her mother's bed and launder the linens. Josie's heart sunk at the thought of her Mama, a lump formed in her throat. She steadied herself a moment looking into her coffee cup like there was a solution to death at the bottom of the cup. Taking a deep breath, she thought, "Might as well do the laundry if I am going to heat water and drag out the washtubs." It wasn't going to do her any good pining away for Mama. Josie needed just to go on, just like her Mama would. Her Ma was such a strong lady in the face of tragedy or hardship. This internal strength was something Josie always admired about her Ma. Josie thought, "I will show her my love through my strength." Just that one thought her Ma almost enlisted a wave of self-forbidden tears.

***

Josie's Journey: Trail of Change

It was lonely there at the farm without Mama. Josie found herself reading and rereading Pa's letters from Fort Laramie. Josie's favorite letter from him she read until she could recite the words.

My darling Mary and Josie,

I have made it to the proverbial land of milk and honey. The journey was arduous but filled with sights that make a man take delight in the Creator. The game is plentiful, and the wind is never-ending, just the thing to fill my Josie's sails. The eyes will never want for beauty in this new territory!

I plan to speak to those in charge at the military installment at Fort Laramie with assistants filling a land patent. There are no near-land offices closer than Kansas. Soon we will have a new home and ranch in this gorgeous wild country. Mary, now you will have the home of your dreams, and I will no longer be gone to work for long months on the river. We will have the life we have worked so hard to have.

I love you, my strong ladies. We shall be together before long as a family on our ranch.

Your loving husband and
Pa,

Jefferson H. Tormey

She missed her Pa also. The house didn't feel the same without her parents. Josie would sit in the silent library reading by candlelight at night, listening to the popping and creaking of the house. She had never noticed those sounds when her parents were at home with her. It had crossed her mind more once that maybe she should go to Pa in Fort Laramie rather than be alone. Then Josie would always come to the same conclusion: she belonged here at home until Pa came for her. She had everything she needed here at the farm to be fine. Besides, wonder if her Pa came for her and she was on her way there to him?

Christmas came and went in lonely isolation. The only companionship Josie had was the animals that she cared for daily. She would spend more time in the barn doing little things than was needed, talking to the cows, horses, donkeys, or chickens. There wasn't a piece of equipment that wasn't in tip-top shape out there. She probably had the cleanest barn in the county, if not state. Josie had never minded being so far from neighbors before

Ma died because she had someone to talk to or just be present. Lonely described her state of being. She would adapt.

It was a gray sleety January day in 1861, almost two months since Ma died when Big Mike docked. She had only a few passing boats stop for eggs, butter, and cheese, but they didn't visit any, which isn't uncommon in the winter. Big Mike's overly tall, robust frame was swiftly moving when he came up the path to the house. It was apparent he was in a fret. His long golden-brown curly hair was sticking in every direction, and he was puffing on his pipe franticly. Josie walked down the path to greet him. Before she could say a word…

"Is your father home yet?" Mike asked, his eyebrows furrowed. He didn't even take time for a greeting

Josie nodded no while giving Big Mike a quizzical look.

"Then I better speak to your Ma," he said, grimacing.

Josie slowly said, "Ma died two months ago. It is just me here."

There was an awkward silence as Mike raked his nervous hands through his wild curls.

"Do you have any coffee?" he asked, looking worried and pale.

They went into the warm, cheery, and inviting kitchen. The stove kept the whole house warm. Ma had been proud of her cast iron stove; it had an oven, not just the top burners. Josie blinked away the memory of her Ma standing next to the stove. The coffee was already on and ready. She took down two blue enamel metal cups and looked at Big Mike, who was usually jovial was now under a gray cloud of discontent, and it was too blatantly obvious to conceal. Maybe, he needs supplies and didn't have trade because something went wrong, Josie speculated. She could help him; with it being just her here at the farm, she had plenty of extra supplies.

"Mike, if it supplies you need and don't have trade, don't worry about it. Your like family. We take care of each other." Josie said this with a big warm smile, hoping to ease Big Mike's discomfort.

The generosity of Josie's offer was not lost. It warmed Big Mike's heart, especially knowing that she was a girl on her own. Big Mike didn't want to

burden the young girl with what he had to say, but it looked like he would have to because her parents were gone.

"Josie, you're a smart, educated girl, and I know you read the papers."

"I always read the papers when I can get them, Mike. Did you bring me any?"

"Not this time...I am sure you have been following the stories on 'Bloody Kansas' for the last few years and the debate to be a slave state or a free state. For years there has been some terrible fighting over in Kansas. Violent...bloody...completely awful guerilla warfare not caring what side of slavery decision people stand on ...just raiding and burning." Shaking his head in disgust.

"I have read about some of this in the papers. The papers seem negligent in telling the whole story and how violent and bad it is there in Kansas. That is what I gather from what you are saying, Mike."

"Newspapers are caught either supporting slavery or against it. We get the *St. Louis Republican*. It is a Missouri paper. Missouri is a slave state. It will print the news to appease slave owners and leave out the rest. I talk to people on the river, and I hear what is going on from people who have been there, and it isn't pretty."

"Is this what has you so upset, Mike? Pa told me after the Lincoln-Douglas debate in Quincy in '58 that newspapers, that is the majority of newspapers, print things one-sided. The press wants to sway public opinion by omitting facts or making one person look better than the other rather than just letting us know the straightforward truth of things. He said it had to do with power and position." Josie studied him with big eyes as she explained what she knew.

"Your pa was right about the newspapers. This situation is substantially bigger than the papers. Josie, the country is building up to war over state rights. You were there for that Lincoln-Douglas debate. Don't you remember slavery was the hot topic of the discourse? When Dread Scott sued for his freedom, that got everyone talking in this country about freed slaves. Slavery has been a bone of contention since this country was founded, and it just keeps on being dealt with one failed agreement or another.

This oncoming war has been brewing for some time, but things are getting mighty tense with this new president coming into office. Some Southern states have succeeded and formed the Confederate States of America right after Lincoln was elected. Some people think war can still be avoided. I am doubtful. I am trying to build up to say that it isn't going to be safe to live here much longer. The Mississippi is a major waterway and the Union, and the Confederates will be fighting to control it for supplies and troops."

"I just won't take sides in this war. Then I will be safe," Josie snapped quickly.

"Josie, even if you remain neutral, neither side is going to care. This place is on the river, and they will force you out…and they won't be nice about it. War is cruel and bloody." Mike said these words, looking in her eyes with a hard-serious stare.

"I know your right. I have studied enough on various wars to know that everyone and everything in a war's path is in danger. We have been at war since the inception of our country with one population or another. Why do Americans want to fight each other? Haven't we had enough fighting?

I have always been disgusted by this slavery topic. People are people no matter what color they are, and they all deserve to be free. I am just so… so… I do know." Josie pauses and swirls her coffee cup, lost in thought. "But this is all I have. What will I do? Pa is out West. Ma is dead." Inside she felt sick and scared. The confidence gained these last few months living on her own now disappeared, and she felt every bit the little girl.

"Josie, I can't tell you what to do. You're in a difficult situation as a girl on your own with a farm to worry about, and me giving you an overwhelming bit of news. I had to make a hard decision for myself when looking at the map of events. I've spent most of my life on the river now I am selling out before this war hits. I sold out my stores in New Orleans already, selling out my stores in St. Louis. I am even selling my beloved boat. Then I am joining a wagon train out west to the goldfields. I have to be in Independence, Missouri the first of April. The wagons start leaving the middle of that month to make their trek out West."

There was a momentary silence while they drank their coffee. Josie's heart was racing. She wanted her Pa desperately.

Josie's Journey: Trail of Change

"Mike, do you think you could help me sell out? All the extra food, the furniture, the stove, quilts, all it. Everything you see. I could sell out just like you." The words came out suddenly.

"What are you thinking about doing then, Josie?" Mike tipped back in his chair and raised an eyebrow.

"The last letter we received from Pa said he was looking for a place by Fort Laramie. I could go to Pa and get out of this mess. I could ride the horse and take a pack mule." This conversation with Mike was the catalyst she needed to go to her Pa.

"I could help you sell out, but that trip is pretty dangerous. There are Indians and road agents. You could get hurt or sick. Yet, I have a feeling staying here is going to be just as bad or worse. More than likely a lot worst." Mike took a deep breath and gave Josie a thoughtful look. He loved this little girl.

"If I start selling out right now, then come April, I will be ready to leave. What do I need to pay you for your help?" Mike hadn't said he would help, but deep down, she didn't think he would leave her to figure things out on her own.

"Some cheese…we're family." Big Mike said with a wink.

The remainder of Mike's visit was busy loading up his boat to the brim with anything that could be sold. It would take a couple more loads before Josie had the household liquidated. One doesn't think about everything they own until they are getting rid of it all. Some things are easy to part with, like a shovel. Her mother's quilts and her family's library were difficult. Ma's stitch work was beautiful; every stitch was placed perfectly spaced, and the designs were colorful, happy like sunsets and flower gardens. Then the books had been her friends have read them over and over again. Ma and Pa talked with her in quiet hours about the finer points of the books. About what was their more significant meaning in the reality of world perspective. Books were to teach us to think and understand. However, a few were strictly to instruct. They have a book detailing medical procedures, surgery, and medical ailments that were just plain useful. Josie had read that book probably a half-dozen times because she found it fascinating.

CHAPTER THREE: PREPARATIONS

Pa and Ma talked about going out West for as long as she could remember. The reason that Pa often worked away from home wasn't just his profession. It was to save for the move to the West. Pa could build lovely things with his hands. Pa had been a shipwright that traveled up and down the Mississippi, masterfully building ships and steamers. He understood wood and how to make it reach its ultimate potential. Pa had stacks of drawings of various vessels and steamers that he designed and built. When Josie was little, she used to look at every ship and steamer on the river and wonder if her father had made it?

She and Ma always stayed home trading their eggs and cheese, but greens in the summer and extra meat when her hunting was good. Somehow the trading and what they provided for their selves left little need. Trading freed most of Pa's money to go to *Boatman's Bank* in St. Louis. Uncle Tom, who had a bank in Quincy, was terribly upset that Pa didn't deposit with him. Pa made up an excuse about convenience. Josie always figured it was something more. A few years prior, she had heard bits about banks folding, but banks weren't something she was familiar with other than a little peripheral knowledge. It did no good for Josie to think of the money in the bank in St. Louis because Pa probably took it West, and if it was in the bank, Josie couldn't get it out if she tried. Josie would be going west with whatever could be gleaned from selling out.

"Clothes would be essential for the journey," Josie thought while forking hay to the livestock. The dress that she was wearing now was bursting at the seams. She didn't want to buy any yard goods to make dresses. She was trying to conserve every cent for what lay ahead of her. Josie would continue to feed the animals and collect the eggs while pondering a clothing solution. She found that thinking sometimes came easier while working. Her mind continued to roll the clothing situation over in her head as she cleaned out the stalls and did a half-a-dozen other odd jobs in the barn.

Josie's Journey: Trail of Change

Cold and tired, Josie decided to go inside and have a cup of coffee; while sitting at the table, the solution to her problem unfolded as she daydreamed at her mother's tea towel. She could use her Ma's things. Josie still had Mama's dresses with a bit of work; they could be modified to fit her. The attire should be made a little bigger than she was now, maybe with pleats so they could be let out as she grew. She could use some sheets to make some new underclothes. Josie was not as handy with a needle as her mother, but her stitch work was still considered better than most individuals. She jumped up flung open the wardrobe studying the dresses with earnest while fingering the cotton dresses on the pegs. Josie continued to think of the modifications the dresses would need. The pocket for the derringer that Ma already made would come in handy. A long open pocket on the other side of the dress for her Bowie knife could be added easily enough. Josie had to remember she was alone, and those simple modifications to her dress may be life-saving. Getting to her knife would be a little awkward, but it would still be there in its sheath. Josie noted to herself that she the need to start carrying Mama's derringer. She already carried her Bowie.

Josie's Journey: Trail of Change

Josie turned from the wardrobe then looked in the mirror at herself in a self-assessing way. She studied her long black braids, big blue eyes with a spray of freckles across her nose. Josie was about five foot two now, almost as tall as her Mama. What a growth spurt she has had these last few months! It was the middle of winter, and her summer tan lines were still vivid. She knew girls were supposed to keep cover to try to stay pale because it was fashionable. She didn't care one stick for fashion; those girls that worry about fashion just aren't living life. How do you hunt with a bonnet? You don't. They have never swum in a pond on a hot summer day. Or allowed a sunrise to warm their face. These are the other reasons to go West, so she doesn't have to live… so confined. This freedom is probably why Pa and Ma wanted to go West in the first place. They were more progressive in their thoughts and beliefs. Progressive thinking doesn't belong to Illinois in the least.

Take the Mormons for an example; they made their trek out West from Nauvoo to avoid religious persecution. Those poor people were driven out of Ohio, Missouri, and Nauvoo, Illinois, because they believed differently from their neighbors. All they wanted was to be free to live their own way of life like people that followed their beliefs. Now those Mormons lived in the Utah territory away from Eastern ideals. Josie didn't know enough about their Mormon beliefs to agree or disagree with them. What she did know was they had a right to their ideas. The Mormons shouldn't have had to go West to find religious freedom. The Constitution was there to protect people's religious beliefs and people's rights as equals.

The Constitution failed because other people didn't heed the document. What did this "failure to heed" get us as a country? The Mormon Exodus and standing on the cusp of war with ourselves. Thinking of all the hatred in the country made Josie feel sick inside and longing to do something to change the world for the better. What could she do she was only thirteen?

Josie's thought drifted back to the West. Will the people out West respect the Constitution? Will she belong out West? Josie never liked going to town because of how people looked and whispered. Hopefully, Fort Laramie is more like our river boatmen. Our riverboat men are a bit course, yet respectful, hardworking, and honest. This general rule respect doesn't mean they haven't chased off a few yellow-belly scoundrels. She wanted to fit into society but didn't want to change who she was to do so. Her parents had raised her well, and she liked herself.

No matter where you live, there are certain unchanging factors like meeting your everyday needs to survive: shelter, food, clothing, fire, water. Then there was the secondary need: society and all that comes with it. For people to work within a community, there are rules, governments, religions, and varying responsibilities delegated to members of that society. Each society sets its rules. The West's rules would surely be different than here. Josie needed to focus on her basic needs for survival to make this journey over the trail. She continued to ponder on society while collecting her items to begin the alterations on the clothing. Her mind would wander, thinking of other great civilizations like the Greeks and Romans.

***

Josie had been staring at the hides knowing that she needed to make herself several new pairs of moccasins but had never been as good as Ma at making them, so she procrastinated as if they would magically appear. This day was the day.

Josie must have new moccasins for the trip; there was no way around it. The ones she was wearing were too small and had large holes in them. She and Ma had tanned several hides last summer in preparation to make moccasin this winter. Josie had never had a pair of store-bought shoes. Every winter Ma made her new moccasins then, as she got older, taught her how to make moccasins. The morning chores were done. She drank her coffee and traced out her moccasin in a larger size on the hide. Then took out her Bowie knife and cut out the pattern. So far, so good…now seven more to go and then to stitch them up with sinew. She would also need to make a document pouch, a money bag, and carrying straps from the tanned leather.

A pile of everything that was going to be taken out West began to form in the place where Ma's bed used to be. This area served as a weigh station of sorts. Josie could study items then and make the hard decisions to take or sell. She could only take necessities. The family bible was considered a luxury item but a record book. This book had traveled back and forth to the pile several times. Ultimately, she decided it would go because documents were a necessary item. The only other book to go would be the medical book, *Western Journal of Medicine and Surgery,* because it could save a life. It was also necessary to take cookware for two, so it looks like she was traveling with someone. The pile kept getting bigger every time she looked: two canteens, Dutch oven, skillet, coffee pot, two bedrolls, seeds for a kitchen garden, jerky, coffee, flour, salt, cold flour, dried vegetables, dried fruit, shovel, ax. Josie knew without a doubt there would be additional items, but this was just the start. No matter how small, she needed to justify carrying it across the country with every item.

Josie found a book on traveling the Oregon Trail by Lansford Hastings in her Pa's things in his desk. She read it several times to ensure she extracted every bit of helpful information out of it. Some of the information was not relevant to her because she would be traveling by horseback and not by wagon. There was useful information, however, to discern from the book. One section of the book stated that it would take the wagon train about two months to reach Fort Laramie. If that was the case, she should at least be able to make it in six weeks by horseback. The book said there

still was some game but not to rely on it. It would be essential to pack enough supplies.

The book noted there were hostile Indians on the trail. She didn't know how much merit to give this statement because the book also said, "all Indians were savages." Her mother wasn't a savage, and neither was she. The one thing the book made mentioned that had her seriously concerned was river crossings. Growing up on the river, Josie knew how unpredictable and dangerous a river might be. The majority of the book was general knowledge to her, but she grew up on the frontier's edge. However, there were a few new things to keep in mind that would come in handy. After pouring over this book several times, the thought crossed her mind about the Donner Party. What books advice had they followed that led to their predicament? Maybe she should rely on common sense more than the book.

The river crossings were a daunting thought and significant concern to Josie. Traveling in the spring would be when the rivers were at their highest means currents would be stronger. Rivers would be deeper. Josie could try to swim the river with her pack train but could easily lose her animals. No, she would have to sacrifice the money to take the ferries. It would cost her more money to replace one lost animal than just take the ferries. The pack train could swim the little streams they would encounter without any problems. Better to avoid risks when possible. Rivers were a considerable risk between currents, quicksand, and slippery embankments; taking the ferries could reduce several mishaps. "It was better to spend a little money to save more money in the long run," Josie thought, reassuring herself this was the best choice

The house was so empty now. It's strange how an empty house can seem even quieter than it was before removing everything. Big Mike took the furniture and all the household items to St. Louis to sell. Mother's kitchen stove was even sold, now the house was heated with the fireplace behind the stove. That is how her parents cooked and heated it before Mama got her stove. The home that her parents built here was just a shell. The barn was no different from the house as far as belongings went. Everything there was gone. The only things left here at the farm were the few things she needed to make the trip or take care of day-to-day routines. She and her mother were always doing little things to make the home more comfortable. Now she just undid all that hard work in a short amount of time.

She was doing the opposite and deconstructing all things to a minimum. It was stunning to Josie how long it took her family to create their home on the river and how extremely fast she sold everything, undoing years of hard work.

A feeling that she had somehow let her parents down by selling out would occasionally flutter into her brain. No, there was no choice. She had to leave. After the war, they could always come back if they wanted. "Besides, Ma and Pa have been saving for years to move out West and start a ranch," Josie would remind herself, "They were going to leave eventually." Knowing this still didn't change her heart from feeling heavy. This place was the only home Josie had ever known. She was born here. Pa always said, "Life is about growth and change." This move was going to be a profound change.

The idea of this journey was scary; she was only thirteen. Thirteen was not really that young, and Josie knew it. Boys as young as nine shipped out as cabin boys or were apprenticed out. Children were forced to leave the orphanages at twelve-she was a year past that. It wasn't uncommon to be married on the frontier at fifteen. Fifteen, and she could be responsible for a family. Pocahontas was only twelve when she saved John Smith and one-hundred sailors from death. Who else was young that had done great things, she thought while lying in bed? Sacagawea was seventeen and had a baby when she helped Lewis and Clark on their expedition. At sixteen, Catharine the Great was Empress of Russia and was regaled for her foreign policy, education, land expansion, legal change, infrastructure improvements…overall enlightenment. Joan of Arc was only sixteen when she helped the French defeat the British. Pope Benedict IX was only twelve when canonized. No, thirteen wasn't so young. She could make this journey. It became a game for Josie to imagine all the other young people in history starting out on their journeys.

***

Managing to get to Fort Laramie safely would rely on appearance. It was important to look like two people were traveling. Feigning someone else's appearance with her would make it possible to stop and buy supplies, if needed, and not be in so much danger. Hopefully, she would have enough to get through the journey and just avoid people. There was still the chance of someone coming along on the trail, though. Taking both horses and saddling them like two riders would be part of the illusion. Then both sets of saddle bags could be packed in also. Studying the supplies that she would be taking with her, she decided to take both mules to carry the supplies. It was possible to pack everything on one mule, but it would tire out easy. If taking both horses and both mules... why not the Jerseys? This ensemble was starting to look like a pack train. If it was a pack train, might as well rig a couple of chicken cages on the Jerseys from old pack saddles. Traveling without a wagon would still mean traveling faster, even with her pack train. Maybe the Jerseys should be left behind...no, they were Pa's gift to Ma.

Josie went over these plans a hundred times in her head. Planning was going to be the key to her safe journey to Pa. Planning is what Ma taught her from the time she could remember—always planning food storage, planning planting, planning chores. There was short-term planning and long-term planning; both had to be done. If they were not done correctly, something or someone suffered. Quickly a person learns to plan accordingly. A person understands what is needed to comfortably get through a winter in food storage. Then always prepare extra food because you never know what

can happen. "Plan for the unexpected," her Ma had told her when doing chores. A task you expect to go quickly can sometimes take all day. Mama was very strict about not procrastinating on tasks because of the unexpected. She was a skillful planner of time and resources. Pa was a planner also. He managed his time well when home. He would take care of whatever chores needed to be done. Do additional building. Manage the household paperwork. Every morning, he would get up then and plan his day with Ma according to what she needed and the most pressing matter. They were so good in their planning that there was always time to read and educate her on varying subjects. Then again, that could have been part of their plan all along.

Josie wandered the eerily silent house aimlessly while it snowed, hoping that she was making the right choices. There was an endless amount of decisions to be made to make this trip come to fruition. The majority of those choices were settled. The only thing to do now was move forward with final plans and take care of daily chores.

The fabrication of the four chicken cages took her several weeks because they had to be fitted to old pack saddles. A plan had to be made to carry their scratch on the Jerseys without the chickens getting into also. It was a time-consuming process weaving the willow branches into cages that would accommodate each bird. While out in the barn, everything for the trip was checked to see if it needed repair. She knew everything was in good repair with all the extra hours she spent in the barn this winter with her animals. However, she still found herself checking the equipment repeatedly as if something might change or happen to it while stored securely in the barn. The combination of the anxiety of the trip ahead and cabin fever caused her to fret about her equipment.

***

Josie's nights had been restless as the days grew slightly warmer. Big Mike's boat docked in the middle of March on a drizzly cold day. Josie was overjoyed to see him. This winter has been the longest she had ever known. When Josie saw his boat, she lit a shuck down the path like her tail was on fire. The smile on her face was from ear to ear.

"My Josie, you sure have grown!" he threw his arms around her and lifted her in a big embrace.

"Mike, it is nice to see you. I have missed you. Come in and have some coffee," Josie said, eyes sparkling in happiness.

The kitchen was warm and smelt of freshly brewed coffee, an inviting reception from the mist outside. Mike and Josie sat down on some logs that Josie had drug into use as chairs around a few more logs to use as a make-shift table. Mike pulled out a copy of the *St. Louis Republican* from his coat pocket. Josie put the coffee down on the make-shift table and sat down.

"Josie, my girl, we sold out just in time. Things are getting worse in this country. Since Lincoln's angulation, more states have joined the Confederated States of America, raising tensions higher. Everywhere you go nowadays, people are arguing about slavery. I suppose if you lived far North or far South, there might not be so many neighbors fighting with each other, but we live in the middle. The middle is in a state of bedlam right now. The middle of this country is where people came from both the North and the South to settle. Abolitionists and slave owners next door to one another. It has got to where people who have been neighbors for years are fighting each other. I am right scared to voice my political view because of

the problems it could cause me. People are getting pushy about knowing if you stand with the Union or the Confederacy. Right here in this newspaper, it tells of people burning other people's homes down because of different political views. People's homes and businesses getting raided all over the slavery issue."

"Which side Union or Confederate, are burning down the houses and doing the raiding?"

"That's the thing, Josie; both sides are credited with burning down houses and doing the raiding. Not only that, but extremists are starting to loot some of the wealthier down in St. Louis. Right there in the city. It is only a matter of time before things get worse from here. Some crooks are taking advantage of the situation to rob and murder people underneath the guise of loyalist feelings one way or the other. I don't know what Congress and the President will do about this civil unrest. They will need to do something quickly because things get worse daily.

The other big thing that is going on in the country that is causing this dissension is economic concerns. People are worried that the banks will fail like some did a few years ago. The government wants a federal banking system to prevent this from happening again. The third puzzle piece is that the abolitionist movement is really riled up about women's rights. They wanted the slaves freed and women to have equal rights. All in one big swoop," Mike shook his head in disbelief.

"As a woman, I want equal rights. I also want an end to slavery. I think that all people should be treated equally. I don't feel that the color of skin or gender has anything to do with the ability to think or feel. However, I am not sure adding another issue to the festering issue of slavery right now is the wisest decision. The issue of women's rights can be handled at a less pressing time. I support the idea of a federal banking system it unifies currency. It also prevents the printing of worthless paper drafts by banks. Unified banking was something Pa and I had spoken about before when all those banks closed because I didn't understand. He also explained that gold was the oldest currency. If we go to war with ourselves, this will cost quite a bit of money, and Congress will have several meetings to figure out funding. I think they will vote some were along the line if we go to war to go to a national currency as a way to stabilize

the economy during all the commotion of war. Mike, what do you think?"

"I have met some savvy women on the river during my years working up and down doing business. Without a doubt, I believe a woman should have equal rights. Maybe some people don't see the strength and wisdom that I have been privileged to see over the years. I have witnessed hard-working women lose everything they own because they were not men, and it isn't right. I have seen women denied an education because they are women and don't study those kinds of things. But a man who isn't half as bright gets the chance to learn the same subject. It isn't right. All of you women live here in the United States and are governed by the same people the men are. You should have a voice in voting people into office.

No man should be a slave. Everyman should be free. I was just a young buck of sixteen and was in the military when I was sent to Georgia '38 to remove the Cherokee people from their homes and march them to Indian territory. It was heart retching! People were pulled from their homes without the chance to change their clothes to weather-appropriate ones. Some people didn't even have shoes. Women, children, elderly, sick no matter they were all marching, without being given so much as a chance to grab provisions for the trip. Some soldiers brutally hit, kick, and even shoot these defenseless people. I was ordered to march the group to the fort while more Cherokee was collected from the area. At the fort, they were treated worse than most people would treat their dogs. It was dirty; people were hungry. I couldn't do anything other than try to be kind while doing my duties. That eviction of the Cherokee people created an indelible image in my mind of the injustice of slavery. My superiors said they were just being moved. I watched as all their rights were stripped away. It was horrid. 'If this is what I watched the Indian go through briefly, what of the negroes?' I remember asking myself that question.

The government will have to do something to fund this upcoming war. Unless they just let the Confederacy stand on its own. I think dividing our country would be a mistake. Besides, we still have the debt of paying Mexico for the territory we bought from them when we won the Mexican War in '48. Texas is one of the states that succeeded. United we stand, united we fall, isn't that how it works? As for currency, I don't have an opinion

other than I like gold. I have always preferred to trade in gold currency."

"That had to be a horrible thing to see and feel so helpless to do anything for the Cherokees," Josie's eyes were downcast. Empathy surged through her for a tribe that could as easily have been her own.

"Before I forget, here is your money. I got $827 for everything, not a bad haul. We could only get a fraction of that in a few weeks from now. With all the political uprising, everyone will want to sell out. I don't need to tell you that this is a lot of money- more than most men make in several years. You don't tell anyone how much you have either… ever. I would put a small amount where you can get to it easy, then cache the rest on you. If a person even thought you had a small amount of money, you could be in danger. Honest people might be tempted to rob or kill you for the amount of money you'll be carrying out West. Don't put yourself in a situation where someone will search your belongings and may come upon your cache. It may be tempting to trust someone on the trail, but don't you have too much to lose, namingly, your life. When you get to your Pa's, find a place to cache your money. Find a place that no one will think to look if, for some reason, you're robbed.

That way, you always have money. A girl should always look to put some money aside for a rainy day," Mike winked at Josie as he told her the last part.

"I will be leaving as soon as I get back to St. Louis. I already have the boat sold and bought a horse. I have made arrangements to pick up my wagon in Independence. Josie, wouldn't you consider changing your plans and coming with me out West? I know we already had this conversation… I just don't feel right leaving you. I've known you your whole life since you were a wee little baby. You don't watch a babe grow into a beautiful young woman and not love and care for her. You and your family have been the only family I have had for years. I knew the second that I docked that I was welcome like I was kin. Your Pa and I would talk for hours, so would your Ma and I. How many meals have we shared in this kitchen? I'd take care of you as if you were my own. I would make sure you got to your Pa then; I could go about my business. Besides, it would be nice to see your Pa. He has been like a brother to me over the years. Please, Josie, reconsider," Mike's eyes were pleading with Josie.

"No, Mike, I have made my plans to take my little pack train. I will be fine. I will be with my Pa before you know it…before your big old prairie schoonin' wagon could get there. Besides, you don't need some irritating little girl pestering you halfway across the country. I'm such an awful girl with a rattle snake streak. No road agents or anyone will bother me all the way to Fort Laramie," said joking to reassure Mike.

"I don't think you're so awful. If you made your mind up, I guess I can't change it. Maybe I will see you out West sometime?" looking at her sadly.

"Mike, you don't have to go yet."

Mike didn't leave until they drained the coffee pot and one more for good measure. Josie thought she had seen tears in his eyes when he turned to walk back down to the boat. It could just have been because she wanted to cry. He had always been part of her life here. Mike had helped her prepare to leave. Now he was gone and didn't know if she would ever see him again. At least her last memory of him was alive, not like the last memory of Mama… dead in a hole. Josie closed her eyes took a deep breath.

CHAPTER FOUR: DEPARTURE

Josie was glad that her family had seldom gone to town after Big Mike told her about the politically motivated raids and the houses getting burned down. Being out of mind would mean that people would be less likely to think of the Tormey Farm when creating mayhem. Josie hoped that because they weren't well known around Quincy, this could work in her favor and not draw unnecessary attention. When her family had gone to town, they spoke to no one other than general pleasantries then, bought their supplies, and left. Unless they had to visit Aunt Susan, their family drew little attention to themselves and lived in a secluded valley next to the river. This life of semi-seclusion could be the lifesaving element Josie needed until she left. She needed to avoid the radical Union or Confederate groups spreading pandemonium. If

she could only remain at home in peace until April...

April did finally arrive with the gift of sunshine and new growth. Josie watching the steady improvement in the weather, decided it was about time to hit the trail. She needed to speak to her neighbor, Sam. Josie saddled her horse then made her way along a winding path hidden from the main road. For as long as she could remember, her family and Sam's had been using this shortcut. She carefully skirted a stand of willows that she knew had a nice cool spring. "I would sure like to stop at the spring. But, every darn spring and fall, those pesky cottonmouths take it over, and I don't have time to deal with them," Josie said aloud to her horse as if it completely understood the whole of her words. She came out of the thicket and could see the smoke from Sam's chimney. Sam was out in the field with his children prepping it for planting.

Josie waved, "Hello, Sam. I got some business to talk if you're not too busy."

"The only business I am ready for at this moment is a hot cup of coffee. Why don't you come

inside?" Sam said as he rubbed his hands together to get off the mud.

"I don't mind if I do," as Josie said this, she dismounted.

Sam walked to the wash bucket by the porch cleaning his hands as Josie hitched her horse to the porch.

"Ma, Josie's here put on some coffee," Sam hollered into the house.

The door opened to the humble farmhouse, "Well, I'll be...you have grown like a willow during a flood Josie," Ma Mary, as everyone called her, hugged Josie, "You get in here and tell us about your winter. Have you heard from your Pa?"

Josie pulled up a chair to the table and sat down, "I haven't heard from Pa in some time. As a matter of fact, that is related to why I am here on business," she graciously accepted a cup of coffee.

"Josie, we haven't heard anything from your Pa. If that is what you wanted to know," Sam said with a serious expression.

"We have been worried about you all winter with your Mama gone, but we didn't want to bother you in your grief. We weren't sure if you went to live with that highfalutin kin of yours over in Quincy either. I couldn't get over this winter due to my condition. Sam, he won't leave my side after the problems with the last young one," Ma said.

Josie related to what Ma Mary was speaking. The winter before last her, Ma was called to aid Sam's wife, Mary. Sam had found her passed out on the floor bleeding. Josie's mama saved Ma Mary but not the baby. It was a difficult loss for Sam's family. It was a miracle that Ma Mary didn't die; there was so much blood! Her mother had told Josie when they went home, "At times, we need to count our blessings when looking at our sorrows."

"I managed fine at the farm through the winter. It was awfully quiet without my Ma," Josie said. "I don't know if you have heard about all this uprising between the Confederates and the Union?"

"We have heard pieces from neighbors and travelers, but we are news starved. We haven't been to town all winter," Sam said.

Josie reached into her large apron pocket and pulled out some clippings, "Well, I figured you might be, so I brought you these articles from the

St. Louis paper. After you read them later, it probably helps make sense of what I am about to say. I am going West to my Pa. I decided that my best option was to sell out, so that is what I did."

"You did what? Don't you think that was a bit like putting the cart before the horse? Your Pa will be home soon enough," Ma Mary blurted out.

While leaning back in his chair, Sam was already skimming the clippings, "Now Ma Mary, I'm looking at some of these articles. Maybe she has her horse and cart in the right order."

"I had to make a tough decision. My parents always planned to move out West anyway. I figured that this problem just forced the moving date. I am planning on leaving in a few days. I sold most everything already other than what I am taking. There are a few odds and ends left at my old house you might find useful. There are also several good laying hens. I just can't take them with me. You folks have been good neighbors to us. I thought you would like what was left."

"Thank you, Josie, but we couldn't just take your things…" Ma Mary said.

"You're not taking them; I am giving them to you. You just have to go fetch the goods after I leave."

The conversation continued about Josie's plans then ended with Josie promising to write from Fort Laramie.

****

Josie was leaving in the morning for Quincy. There was a ferry there that could take the pack train across the river. The thought had glanced across Josie's mind about going down to St. Louis and taking a ferry there instead, but she decided against it. The trip to St. Louis would mean a lot of extra miles and go into a big city with everyone feuding. That wasn't the logical decision when trying to avoid people and trouble. By tomorrow night, she would be on the West side of the Mississippi.

Her last night at home was restless. Josie walked around the house, studying it from every angle, knowing this was goodbye. There was a queer sensation in her stomach and a lump in her throat the whole time. She felt like she was parting with a piece of herself by leaving the farm. The smell of the river and the fresh spring grass deep down somewhere would always be forever imprinted as the scent of home on the farm. She couldn't turn back from the choices she had already set in motion. However, it didn't change the deep-felt fear bubbling within her. There was so much that could happen in the next few weeks on the way to Pa. People were fighting among themselves over state rights. How would she make it to her father without problems when the country was a hornet's nest of opposing ideas? Traveling the trail itself was going to be hard enough. Yesterday, Josie did a dry run of loading all the gear on the mules and the Jerseys. It took her almost an hour. She was barely strong enough to do the task. Hopefully, she would get stronger every time she loaded. Lying there that night, she staged in her head many different ways how the packs may be situated to make them easier to load and unload. Josie did eventually drift into sleep.

The sky was still the rich inky blue of night when Josie woke and set to making coffee. Only enough coffee for a few more days; however, she was not going into Quincy to buy any. There was too big of a risk of seeing her aunt and uncle if she ventured into a store. The ferry was a big enough risk but one that must be taken. Also, she doubted that either her aunt or uncle would be down by the river. They rather be in town itself; it was more prestigious. Her Aunt would consider the river to be an unseemly place to be. She would just use what she had, then go without coffee until Independence, when supplies could be bought. Then, she drank her coffee and packed up her few kitchen items in a coarse cloth sack. The sky was now streaked with sunlight. Josie's heartfelt heavy, stepping out into the sun-lit yard and closing the house door behind her. The air was clear; you could smell the river, spring grass, the barnyard. The chickens were clucking, and a gentle breeze was blowing. This place was home, or it had been home.

Josie set about milking the Jerseys. It was disturbing to be dumping out the milk. It was against everything she had been taught her whole life to be wasteful. Drink her share, then what else could she do? They were traveling, and the milk could not be stored. At least the chickens would drink some milk while the mules were loaded and the horses saddled. The milk could be counted as part of her meals while getting to Fort Laramie. The milk would mean her food would last longer. The chickens probably wouldn't be laying any

eggs. Chickens are notional creatures; they just don't lay eggs if everything isn't just right.

The pack train was in order. Josie was riding at the forefront of the pack train holding the lead lines of her other horse and the two lines of the Jerseys. She didn't have to worry about lines on the two-pack mules, who she affectionately called the "Jennies," because they would follow her horses anywhere. Mules are incredibly social creatures. Once they decide who their family is, they will stay faithfully with them come rain or shine. Thinking about how often she had seen the Jennies nuzzling her horses out in the pasture over the years brought a smile to her face. That is the way families are supposed to be caring for one another. Families are to stand loyally at one another sides through good and bad. Mules knew the elements to make a strong family. They were wise, loving animals.

The road to Quincy was well established; two evenly worn ruts marked the frequent wagon traffic. It was about seventeen miles to the ferry. The morning was bright and beautiful, the air crisp and smelling fresh like new growth. New vibrant green leaves on the trees marked that spring was finally here after the long winter. They traveled at

about four miles an hour and would arrive at the ferry before noon. To spite the beautiful weather, she had not seen hide nor hair of another traveler on the road this sunny morning. Folks must be taking advantage of the weather to start their planting, she mused to herself. Josie wanted to have the river crossing far behind her before she stopped for the evening. She reasoned the farther away from people, the less likely she and her pack train were to have problems. The fact that there was a ferry in Quincy was a stroke of good luck.

Having a ferry in Quincy would save Josie a lot of unseen problems and time. Pa had told her that Quincy had grown exponentially since Ma and he first built the farm. It is a town of about 13,000 as far as Ma and Josie were concerned that just too many people in one place. Pa was used to large cities because of his work. He didn't think Quincy was too big. New Orleans had about 170,000 people, and St. Louis had about 160,000 people, and that isn't counting all the little towns around those big cities. Quincy was small when looking at Quincy from the perspective of those cities Pa usually worked. Quincy was big enough to warrant a ferry for all the outlying communities on both sides of the river.

The ferry was at the North edge of town. Unfortunately, Josie and her pack train would have to cross part of the riverfront to be on the Northside of the community where the ferry stood. She carefully made her way along the riverfront, diligent not to make any eye contact with anyone. For once, Josie was happy about having a bonnet that could hide her face in the deep confines of the hat's design. Usually, the cotton prairie bonnet dangled precariously by its strings from her neck, never to be worn, but now it was worn out of necessity.

Arriving at the ferry, Josie evaluated the vessel that was to take her and her pack train over the river. She was more than a bit concerned. Ramshackle would be the word to describe the haphazardly built ferry. There were significant gaps in the planking. The wood was silver with age. Here and there, you could see a board pulled loss with the nail protruding. There was only one ferry, and this was the only choice forward. Surveying the scene further, Josie noticed the ferryman. He was thin. His dark brown long overgrown hair was greasy with filth; his clothes were covered in varying degrees of stains and mud. His hands were black with God knows what;

the man hadn't shaved in some time. He wore worn-out store-bought clothes and shoes…not boots. Odd, most working men wore boots. When he spoke, he had a southern draw, and he looked at her like she was a meal to a starving man. Josie didn't like the look of the whole situation at the ferry. What concerned her the most was the look in the ferryman's eyes. The look in his eyes had sent chills up Josie's spine. The sooner she could get over the river and away from him, the better.

While staring at Josie, the ferryman asked, "What can I do you for little missy?" then spit a long stream of tobacco in the dirt.

"I need to get across the river. My Pa is waiting for me there."

"Why didn't he take the livestock and you?" The ferryman drawled, still staring at her with cold black eyes like a predator sizing up their prey's weakness.

"Pa took the boat with all our goods and told me to come along with the stock. He would meet me on the other side. Then we would go on to my grandparents together," She was lying with a straight face while unflinching looking this despicable man in the eyes. Her heart was racing,

and her palms were sweating. She was scared. Besides, Josie was raised not to lie, but here was strung together one mighty lie. She was lying out of self-preservation, she reminded herself.

"How much to go across the river? When can we go across?" Josie asked this with all the courage she could muster. She envisioned how Aunt Susan spoke to people like she was in charge of everything. Josie even used Aunt Susan's tone of voice that dictated authority. Josie didn't dare to show any of the meekness or fear that she was feeling inside.

"It will be fifty cents per animal and a dollar for you. That will be four dollars, little missy," he said this with a gritty yellow smile still staring through those soulless black eyes.

Josie knew that he was charging about double what he would be charging a man, but what was she to do? She had to get across the river. There was not another ferry that she knew of until St. Louis.

Interpreting her momentary silence, the ferryman spoke, "If you don't have the four dollars, maybe we can work out a deal." He licked his lips and

looked her up and down while wiping his filthy hand on his shirt.

Josie knew from that day long ago when Ma had been violated what this man meant. Ma had a long talk with her that day. Yet, she was just a girl. She was starting to round out a little but was far from being a woman. The thought that this man had even had that idea made her want to vomit. Josie could hardly think her heart was pounding so hard, and her stomach was like a bucking horse. She was so nervous and upset. She still needed to get across that river.

"I have the four dollars. I want to go across the river now," Josie said firmly, taking the money from her pouch. The ferry man's disappointment and shock in his eyes were obvious from the way they flickered when Josie produced the money. He had probably never expected a farm girl to pay that kind of money to cross the river.

Reluctantly, the ferryman guided her horses, Jerseys, and mules onto the rickety old ferry. He never said a word more. They slowly made their way across the vast Mississippi River. The river cross-current was tugging at the ferry, causing the deck to heave to and fro. When the deck would shift, the animals would step nervously to re-align their balance. Josie could tell the pack train was anxious to be on solid ground by their uneasy steps and blowing sounds they made. She could not blame her animals one bit. Josie could feel her insides crawling. She wanted to be away from this ferry also. Occasionally when glancing back, Josie caught the ferryman staring at her. It made her cringe; her heart still had not stopped racing, and it felt like crossing the river was taking an eternity. No doubt her mind that if the ferryman thought he could get away with harming her, he would. He wanted something perverse, she believed, because of the way he ogled her with those black sin-filled eyes. There was also the fact that he knew she had some money. She remembered what Mike said about people being willing to rob or kill for money.

Gratefully the ferry eased onto the bank on the opposing side of Quincy. The town was not visible from this side of the river because of a stand of willows and curves in the river, but the bank was firm for docking, allowing easy loading and unloading. Josie slowly began walking the slightly nervous horses forward to disembark from the ferry. The deck was wobbling under their motion.

The Jerseys were following close behind the horses. Josie was intently focused on getting her pack train back on solid land and putting some miles between the river and them. Suddenly, the ferryman jerked up Josie by the back of her dress. She had not seen him coming at her because her bonnet was still on covering her face. Josie was completely shocked by the abrupt action and the jarring fall to the ferry's deck. She jumped up quickly, aware deep inside that the situation was grim. Josie quickly slapped the horses on the rump to get them to run off the ferry. The Jennies then crowded the Jerseys off the ferry to get to the horses in rapid reaction.

During the dismounting of the pack train from the ferry, Josie tried to distance herself from the ferryman. Her action was unsuccessful. The ferryman grabbed her by her arm with an inhumanely strong grip. Using the wobbly conditions of the ferry, Josie pushed into him with all her strength, knocking him off balance. The ferry made a heave to one side as the ferrymen fell. She quickly stepped back, hoping to make a break for the shore when he tripped her. Josie careened down on her side, trying to get up quickly. Her long dress tangled around her legs, slowing her movements. Before she could free her legs, the man was sprawled on top of her holding her wrists. Josie, determined to be free, kneed him in the groin. He rolled to the side, clutching himself in writhing agony. Josie had her feet under her when the ferryman grabbed her braid then pulled her down with a swift hard jerk. Her face smashed onto the deck, causing her nose to erupt in an explosion of blood. Josie was now flat on her belly, trying to scramble away from the man when he grabbed her leg quickly. He then began pulling her closer to him using her leg like a rope. Josie had a delayed reaction on what to do next because her head felt dizzy. She finally came to her senses, turned her body the best she could then, kicked the ferryman in the face with all the strength her awkwardly positioned free leg possessed. He lunged back with the impact causing him to let go of her. Josie went to her feet like a cat, ready to jump up and run. He was also on his feet, already blocking the way to shore.

For a fleeting moment, they just stood there and stared at each other. Josie stared into his soulless black eyes, her heart was racing, and she was breathing hard. A primal chord had been struck within her. The ferryman lunged at her grabbing her throat with one of his massive filthy hands. He was slapping her with his other across the face. Josie tried in vain, prying his hand off her frail neck, but he was too strong. She first began to see spots while fighting the hand at her neck. Then could feel the world starting to grow dark and stop fighting. He dropped her at that moment to the deck when she feigned being unconscious. As the man was choking the life from her, she knew that this man meant to kill her, not just rob her. The ferryman, thinking Josie dead, rolled her over roughly and began to lift her long-entangled dress. Josie slowly eased her hand into the pocket with the derringer, cautious not to draw attention that she was alive. Once the derringer was in her hand, she eased it from her pocket. The man's concentration was on Josie's undergarments. She raised the derringer slowly and took careful aim. The man did know what was happening until he heard the gun cock. By then, it was too late. Josie shot him right between the eyes.

Josie could smell the acrid scent of gun powder and the stench of the unwashed body of the ferryman as the ferryman's body collapsed on top of her. She heaved the ferry man's body off her in with effort and disgust. Shaking, heart racing, and

resisting the urge to vomit was her eternal state at that moment. It was almost too much to bear. Josie had never killed anybody before nor wanted to kill anybody. There was blood all over the front of her dress, face… it was even in her hair. Wanting to cry, she thought, "What was one supposed to do now?" All she had wanted was to cross the river with her pack train. That should not have been complicated. "Now look at this fine mess: I killed a man, blood everywhere, animals gone, hurt." Think logically, one step at a time, and breathe, she told herself, envisioning how her Pa always did this when faced with a challenge. How could she logically think when fighting back tears and shaking uncontrollably? She sat for a moment then, reigned in her fear because that part of this whole debacle was over.

The fear Josie had felt had been exchanged for anger, and it was raging at the ferryman. "It was completely his fault for all this nightmare problem," echoed through her mind as she walked to the corpse of the ferryman. "He was going to rape and kill me," was fuming within her head, even after he got her four dollars. She stood there looking at the shell of the man and wanted to yell at him. Tell him what a low-down rotten skunk he

was, but she couldn't. "Well, I am taking my four dollars back," she said aloud with a tone of triumph. Riffling through his pockets, she found five dollars and fifty cents. He didn't have any personal effects on him. She put the money in her pouch then pushed his miserable body into the vast river.

Feeling a little more composed, Josie went to the riverbank, stripped and washed out her clothes to rid them of all the blood. She bathed her face and had to un-plate her hair to wash out the blood. It was quite the process just to get clean. Her animals had run off, so she didn't have any real soap. Lucky for her, there was some soap weed growing near the river that she used. Feeling dirty mentally, knowing what the ferryman had intended to do to her, she stood washing in the river longer than she needed to. The washing was not getting rid of the disturbing feelings. Josie's thoughts turned towards her mother. Ma must have felt worst after what her uncle did to her. Her mother was so strong, Josie reflected, looking over the expanse of the flowing river. If her mother could be strong, so could she, Josie resolved. Even after washing several times, Josie could still smell the sickening scent of the ferryman's body odor and blood.

After all this nasty business with the ferry was done. Josie had to round up her stock before proceeding on her way. Luckily, they strayed less than a quarter of a mile from where they had docked. The stocks location probably had more to the weight of the packs and the greenness of the grass than luck. Josie was soaked and wet and notably disturbed by killing a man. The sun didn't seem to be drying her fast enough to help blot away the day's event. This day would haunt her dreams. A good part of the day had been lost to the drama at the ferry. Now they needed to make some miles before dark and get away from this dreadful place. Josie made a concerted effort to focus on the scenery while traveling or recited poems aloud. She was doing anything to regain control of her mind and emotions. She had too long of a journey ahead of her to allow this event to take root and destroy her. The remainder of the first day of travel was uneventful. The sun was bright and warm, and the grass was green; a slight gentle breeze stirred now and again. Josie's little pack train was not trail broke yet, so they didn't travel as well as they would be by the time they reached Independence. They required a little coaxing here and there. However, they did a good job, especially for never having traveled any distance before.

Josie was alert, seeking a place to make camp, once she noticed the first streaks of sunset. It was slightly after dark before she found a camping spot. The area that was found was ideal. There was a small trickling creek, no more than two steps wide, with a grove of willow trees around it. Perfect location or not, Josie needed to make camp earlier from now on out on the trail. The Jersey had been gradually bawling louder for the last hour to be milked. They just were going to have to wait their turn. Slowly and stiffly, Josie climbed off her horse, rubbing the neck of her companion. She walked back to the Jennies, took a couple of long lengths of rope off the pack, and built a make-shift pen from trees and rope. Then one by one, Josie took the loads off the Jennies, taking the extra time to rub them down with grass and doing the same for the horses. Lastly, the Jerseys got their much-desired attention because they had to be milked. She placed the chicken cages on the ground and gave them each a little scratch and milk. They began happily pecking at bugs. Finally, after caring for her stock, Josie could care for herself. She was exhausted and wanted coffee but, knowing how little she had, decided against it. She ate a handful of cold flour and drank some milk. What was needed beyond anything else was a good

night's sleep. Josie rolled out her bed role, sougam, and looked at the stars on the plush grass.

The stars above were a new experience; she had never slept outdoors before. In the summer, some time, Josie and Mama would sleep on the porch in hopes of a cool breeze. But that didn't count because the house was right there. There were so many peculiar sounds. She could hear her little pack train chewing the grass nearby, chickens making an occasional happy clucking sound, and the crickets chirping. She could listen to the trickle of the little creek, frogs, an owl, and... the howling of wolves. Maybe she should have started a fire in the camp. The night was warm enough, and she didn't cook anything. The thought of a fire never crossed her mind until she heard the wolves. Would a fire scare off wolves? Josie got out of bed and retrieved her rifle that was beside her saddle. The gun was loaded. During her emotional state today, she had forgotten to re-load the derringer. With a skilled hand, getting her powder and ball from her saddle bag quickly loaded her gun in the moonlight. She then placed both of the guns where she could grab them quickly if the wolves came into her camp. Josie had heard tales of mules and horses fighting wolves when attacked but was not going to risk her livestock or herself. She lay awake for a long time to spite her exhausted state, listening to the sounds of the night before finally drifting into a deep sleep.

CHAPTER FIVE: TRAIL LIFE

The yellow light of morning was barely streaking the sky when Josie awoke abruptly and breathing heavy. Momentarily she forgot where she was; this gave her a burst of adrenaline. Quickly everything was remembered. Her muscle slackened as she relaxed. Lying in her bedroll, she became increasingly aware of feeling everything from the day before, the travel and the beating, as the adrenaline left her body.

Additionally, everything was covered in a light frost this morning. The body objects adamantly against getting out of a nice snug, warm bedroll on a cold morning, but it must be done. Quickly Josie dressed in the chill. Her face was swollen and sore. She contemplated getting the small mirror from her pack and looking at the damage to her face but decided against it. If she saw the damage, it just

might get her all riled up again. She had finally calmed down over the matter. Josie went to the creek and bathed her face in the cold water giving her a little relief. Thinking of how sore she was from traveling, she assumed her stock was also. The only solution to get past the aches and pains and soreness was to keep going. Josie had learned this long-ago doing chores like haying. The only way to get past the pain was to keep working. Eventually, your body builds a tolerance, and you don't hurt anymore. The stock and she would need to build up a tolerance to the trail. In the meantime, it was going to be mighty unpleasant.

Josie milked the Jerseys, drinking her share of the milk. Then started the arduous process of packing all the animals, including watering them well before leaving their camp. Saddling up, chewing on a piece of jerky, determined to have a better day than yesterday, Josie and the pack train began the long trek West. Josie would find herself half dozing in the saddle sometimes as she stared out at the infinite miles of grass in front of her. There were islands of forest to break up the miles of grass. Occasionally there was a farm; however, most of her time was spent gazing at the expanses of grass. This land was just so incredible to see.

Often Pa had a friend stop by to visit in the winter who had been out West, and they spoke of the grasslands before you reach the mountains. Some misguided people call it the *Great American Desert*. Pa always wanted to be near the mountains. Wonder if Fort Laramie is near the mountains? Pa's one friend had said that the grasslands were so extensive you felt like they would never stop. Pa's friends said many people are starting to settle on those grasslands farming, crowding out the Indians. "There is so much land I don't see how anybody could be crowded?" Josie spoke aloud to herself. "Look how many people live in the small space of Quincy. Here there are miles of openness and not a person in sight. It's a good thing that people were farming out here. Farms are important, besides there sure is a lot of grass. The Indians and farmers can just share the land; there looks to be enough for both of them. If there is not enough land, then one of them is just being too greedy."

On more than one occasion, Josie saw a cabin in the distance but kept her distance. After the horrid run-in with the ferryman, she was in no mindset to run into any more trouble. Josie kept to herself no matter how desperately she wanted a nice

satisfying cup of coffee. The pack train and she were becoming hardened to the trail. They easily traveled twenty-five to thirty miles a day. She was also becoming accustomed to the daily routine of unloading and loading the animals. The loading had a rhythm and system in itself. Once gained, the task went quicker. The Jerseys were producing a little less milk, which was expected with all the travel. They were still making more than enough for Josie. Between the milk, wild greens, and wild onions, the packed supplies were being reserved primarily other than the cold flour. She hadn't even put a dent in her stores.

When in Independence, Josie needed to buy a few supplies to get her to Fort Laramie. It was always better to have extra than not enough. A few things were required from the beginning of the trip, but she didn't dare go to Quincy to get them. Realizing that she needed them after it was too late for Big Mike to procure them for her, she set her mind to purchase those items in Independence. Thinking about making a purchase made Josie think about the sizable amount of money she was carrying. Knowing that no one was around to observe anything, she stopped right then and there and shifted her money around. Now with the shift of

funds, there were forty dollars in her pouch to make purchases. The majority of her money was sewn into her underclothes and reinforced with additional fabric. A hook and eye closure inside a pocket on one of the sums for easier access. Big Mike had made it very clear about keeping your money cached.

Josie had been noticing for about the last day more and more farms. More farms were a sure sign of getting closer to Independence. When coming out of a tall grass field, she abruptly structs a well-traveled road and knew that they would be to Independence before the day was out. Glad to be arriving at Independence, but not the time of day. The time meant that she would have to camp near town, near people, and everything to be avoided. If she only knew how far it was to Independence, she could camp on the prairie. However, she didn't know the distance and could very well end up in the same situation tomorrow. Josie hated making uninformed decisions but had no choice in this matter.

With the knowledge of what lay ahead, all she could do was continue forward toward Independence. The sun started to set while coming down the last long curve into Independence. It was

picturesque with the colorful sunset and all the white canvas on the wagons reflecting the colors. The view was littered with miles of wagon trains preparing for their trip West. Further off in the distance was the framed grid-work of a town. The sun continued to set as the pack train made its way to the cusp of wagons. Coming closer to the wagon trains, there was a frenzy of activity, women preparing meals and tending to children. Children were managing stock or playing. Men were huddled together, talking or mending items.

Josie needed a safe spot to camp. After thinking for a moment, she gathered her courage and had made a plan. Whether she could carry it out was yet to be seen. Josie approached the last wagon in a long row where a clean boxomous red head middle-aged woman was cooking dinner, and her children were busy doing various tasks. Sitting back on her horse in the shadows of the trees, Josie watched a while before climbing off her horse. With slow apprehension, cat-like steps, she approached the woman's camp.

"I was just wondering how long you were going to sit there before you came into camp?" the middle-aged woman said with an Irish accent.

"I was scared," Josie answered honestly, not making eye contact.

"Nothing to be scared of here, except me boys; they are a handful," she said with a smile. "What is it that you be needing, dearie?"

"My Pa went on into town and didn't come back yet, and I have to make camp alone, and I am scared. There are so many people," Josie said, staring at the ground.

"That could be quite a problem for a young lass as yourself. You can make your camp by us, dearie, and you will be safe as can be. As for your Pa, nothing can be done tonight. You can set out and find your Pa in the morning then. Everything will be right as rain. There is no sense giving no more worry over these problems this night, dearie," this was said with a joyful smile.

"I have cows. They need to be milked; do you want the milk? I can't drink it all by myself," she asked, stumbling over her words, still looking at the ground, ever scared of being discovered alone.

"Milk will be a fine treat. Here takes our pail," the Irish woman said with a wink.

Josie went about the usual nightly routine with her pack train. Then walked the pail of milk to her host family, as they were. While approaching the light of the campfire, she counted six children and the two parents, all with varying shades of red hair, all eight going West into the unknown. She stopped standing in the shelter of the trees, watching their camp and listening. This view was that of a typical family. Josie had no reason to be the bundle of nerves she was right now.

"Don't be shy back there in the shadows. You're safe here. Here is the little dearie that lost her Pa I was telling you about earlier. What is your name, dearie? Ours be O'Reilly."

"My name is Josie Tormey. I brought you some milk like I said I would," as Josie said this, Mrs. O'Reilly took the bucket of milk with a grateful smile.

"Do you hear that a Tormey? A fellow Irish. We Irish have to help each other. There would be many who would not so much as help an Irishman. Blame the Irish for every wrong in this great country. We are responsible for Cholera, the Blight, and Satan himself. Tis, a hard road an Irishman walks in this country indeed… Sit down,

me girl, and have some stew. Ma makes a fine kettle of stew and the finest biscuits around. Now tell me, lass, where are you and your Pa headed off to? We're headed to Oregon where we will have us a fine farm," Mr. O'Reilly said with a huge dimpled smile on his round face.

"We are going to the Fort Laramie area. Where we are going to ranch."

"Will you be going by wagon train? We could group up and help one another along the way. The best company for an Irish family is another Irish family."

"No, Mrs. O'Reilly, we are going to take our pack animals and make a quicker trip over the trail, at least that is what Pa says," She threw in the part about Pa saying it because she did not want anyone getting the notion that she was alone.

"No one calls me Mrs. O'Reilly...Ma will do," she said with a laugh and a wave of her plump hand.

"If there are only two of you, I suppose a pack train could do you for the travel, but we have a brood. A wagon is almost not enough to contain this family. We'll make it do. It will only be a few

short months before we are in Oregon. Won't it, Pa?"

Josie ate her stew, enjoying every bite. She had been in the habit of making cold camps and not eating a hot meal. This meal was a treat. Ma O'Reilly biscuits were …light, fluffy, and delicious. They were the best she could remember. She sat back content and full while listening as Mr. O'Rielly described the fine farm they would have in Oregon to his family. Josie thought the dream of the Oregon farm was part of every member of this family's soul. After enjoying her savory dinner, she washed her dish, excusing herself to her camp and bed. Josie rolled out her bedroll listening to the night, which had become her habit. The sounds were different near the wagons. There was still the sound of her livestock chewing grass, the sound of a crickets, and she could hear the quiet talk of the people of the wagon train. Josie still slept with her rifle and derringer, never trusting anyone, gradually dozing off while getting acquainted with the sounds.

Josie woke long before the sun had risen. She began to prepare the animals for the day's journey when it dawned on her it would be easier to go into town with only the two horses. Quietly walking into the O'Reilly camp and grabbing the pail used the night before to milk the Jerseys, Josie returned to milk the cows. When bringing the fresh milk to the O'Reilly camp, she saw Ma had coffee on the fire.

"I am sorry if I woke you. I thought you might want the milk," Josie apologized, holding out the pail.

"I was already awake when you got the pail. I am not accustomed to sleeping under the wagon as of yet. Not that I've had a life of luxury but never have I slept outdoors under a wagon until this trip. Then there is always the call of nature to wake one up also. I figured you would like a little coffee since you were a stirring around so early this morning. Coffee helps a person brace the day," she handed her a cup.

"We have been out of coffee for days now. Thank you. Coffee is one of the things we need to get in town today. I was weaned straight onto coffee as a baby, and being without it has been mighty difficult," Josie inhaled the aroma from the cup and was beyond grateful for the generosity.

"I find not having me coffee makes for a rough time and a rougher time for those around me. Was

raised on tea, but once I found coffee, I wanted no more of that. Well, occasionally, a cup of tea if I am sick with a thick lashing of sugar and whiskey. Now that your day is started, what are your plans for today, dearie? Are you going to wait here for your father or go about looking for him?"

"Well, I have made up my mind that I have got to find my Pa and lay in the few supplies that we need to get us to Fort Laramie. I don't want to be without coffee on the trail again. Hopefully, once I find Pa, we can get across the river then, make camp on the other side tonight. This crossing will be the last major river crossing for pa and me. It will feel good to have it over and done with. Those crossings are stressful. It is going to be mighty busy in town with people crowding around getting ready for the trail. I was wondering, Ma, if it would be alright to leave my pack train here while I look for my Pa? It would be a lot easier."

"That is a wise idea, lass. Those streets are a tangle of wagons, oxen, and horses. These huge teams of oxen needed to pull the wagons can quickly make the streets unpassable. Dearie, there is no since dragging those animals of yours through all of the mess of town while you tis looking for your father. You are right. You will get a lot further in your

search if you leave them here. Now, don't you be worrying any; we will be looking out for your stock, dearie."

"Lassie, watch to your safety in town. There be a lot of fine people in town, but there are many that are not so fine. I don't know how familiar you are with cities, dearie. I want you to be mindful while you look for your father. I realize I am not your mother, but as a mother, I cannot help but worry about a pretty young girl. The street they'll be crowded and noisy. It is easy for one to get distracted. Dearie, be paying attention to what you're doing so nothing will be happening to you. When you be going into the stores, don't let them convince you to be buying any more than what you need. Oh, that is one of those sly salesman tricks…get you to be buying extra items. You're a good smart lass. You'll do fine," Ma O'Reilly said, taking a long drink of her coffee.

"Thank you, Ma. I have been into a busy city a few times but never alone. I was raised out in the country on a farm. We traded for what we needed most of the time with people on the river. Because we traded, we didn't need to go to town very often to make purchases. Pa often worked in vast cities, but Ma and I would stay at home on the farm. I

appreciate your words of advice for the heart that they are coming from and love intended," Josie smiled at Ma O'Reilly with appreciative affection, swallowed the last dregs of her much appreciated the coffee, and left to return to her camp.

Back at her camp, Josie combed and re-plaited her hair, washed her face, and dusted her clothes off the best she was capable. Her stock had been tended to earlier in the morning. Still, she hesitated to leave her stock. It felt unnatural to be leaving part of her pack train behind while going to town. They had been together day in and day out for what seemed like forever to Josie. Knowing what needed to be done, she separated the horses from the other animals and saddled them. The Jennies were braying in concern. Stopped what she was doing and scratched the Jennies between the ears with understanding, reassuringly telling them that she would be back soon and their family would be back together before long. Slowly leading the horses away from the multiple close camps near her to raise no commotion. As she approached the road, Josie mounted up and headed into the busy confluence of Independence.

The closer Josie came to town, the more grateful that she had made the decision to leave her pack train at the O'Reilly camp. Josie never imagined so many people trying to crowd into any one place. She had heard her father and Big Mike speak of the crowded, busy streets of St. Louis and New Orleans, but those were just words. Having listened to conversations by Pa and his friends, there were much bigger places back East that had city congestion. Never had she imagined so many people trying to do so much in just a few blocks. It was all that she could do not to stare at all the coming and going of people. Independence was probably a third of the size of Quincy, but she had near seen Quincy even remotely as busy as Independence. The busiest Quincy had ever been that she could remember was the day of the Lincoln-Douglas debate people had come from all around the state. Even then, Quincy was not as chaotic or crowded as the small section of business fronts that she needed to approach. There was no choice; Josie needed her few supplies. She took a deep breath and moved forward.

Josie didn't bother hiding in the confines of her bonnet this day; instead, she let it dangle from her neck as she usually did when away from society. This day, the other girls in town were doing the same thing with their bonnets, allowing them to

hang freely. Besides, if her bonnet was on her head, she might miss something transpiring around her. Plenty was going on around her that needed to be observed for safety's sake. The well-rutted roads were overly crowded with wagons drawn by oxen, as men were loading provisions for the journey west. There were plenty of horses crowding hitching rails in front of stores that sold everything imaginable. Saloons were open, and Josie could hear music and loud arguments coming from within while passing by them. There were dozens of stores with signs hanging above them: cobbler, milliner, seamstress, etc. The boardwalks were full of men and women hustling and bustling to various places. It was overwhelming to Josie as her mind spun and her heart raced from all the noise, people, traffic, and general commotion. All she needed was a simple general store to buy her few odds-and-ends for the trail then, to get out of there with haste. How could people live like this every day, surrounded by never-ending chaos? They did live like this obviously because there were blocks and blocks of houses along with the blocks and blocks of stores.

Josie sat her horse for a moment in the middle of the dusty chaos and watched where the wagons were loading their provision, hoping that would guide her to where she needed to be to buy what was on her trail list. She watched as one burly blonde man load barrels and bags of varying items into his wagon. She decided this was the right place to get her provisions. Tying her horses to the already crowded hitching post, Josie looked up at the sign above the door, which simply read "Goods." She opened the door to the store, and a bell chimed her entrance. The store had the familiar scent of spices and leather. It was crowded in the store. She had to work her way through the throng of people looking at clothes, yard goods, and a dozen other things before making her way to the service counter at the back of the store.

The clerk was busy totaling up some orders; he looked at Josie then resumed his tallies. Then he went about stacking some items. He never verbally acknowledged her presence, but he did make eye contact. Josie told herself, "He must be finishing an order, and I will be helped next," though she was a bit disgusted by his rudeness. Two other people got service that stepped up to the counter after her. She just continued to wait at the counter outwardly patient; however, her blood pressure was beginning to rise at the clerk's continued

rudeness. After the third and fourth people got service, she began to get her ire up. When the store clerk once again began to walk by her again. Josie finally spoke up.

"I believe I am next. I have been waiting some time. Pa is going to get sore. It is taking me so long," She said it loud and clear.

"What do you want… some candy?" the clerk said, condescending.

"No, I do not want any candy," Josie glared at the clerk. "Pa sent me in to get a few items for the trail, and I need them immediately," she said with all the authority of someone who may have owned the store. Josie was fuming with this man's rudeness. At the same time, she was scared and nervous about him refusing to fill the order or asking questions about Pa. Her heart was beating like a humming bird, and the anger had brought a flush to her cheeks.

"Yes, miss, what can I get you?" his tone changed when he realized this was to be a trail purchase.

"I need twenty pounds of coffee, two rain slicker, two large canteens, and twenty pounds of cold

flour. That should do it for my order," Josie quickly snapped.

"You sure you don't need more provision it is a long way over the trail? You and your family don't want to end up like the Donner Party. People often underestimate what they need. We have these things called meat biscuits. A lot of folks are taking them over the trail. Don't require no cooking," the clerk asked with a fake smile, trying to get more of a sell.

"No, we are well stocked. We just needed these few items to round out our supplies."

"May be some hard tack? That is a supply all folks need," the clerk still trying to get more of a sell.

"No, like I said before, I just need those items I asked for the trail," Josie was standing tall and looking the clerk in the eyes when she spoke.

The clerk scratched the list with some number on a tally sheet, then spoke, "That will be seven dollars and twenty-three cents."

"That is a little high priced for what I bought. I, however, need the goods... here you are, sir," she hesitantly handed over the money.

"You're going to find that prices are higher out here. It is the cost of living on the frontier," with those words, the clerk walked off and began stacking her order in front of her on the counter.

Josie loaded her newly acquired provisions on her spare horse. Now on her list was to find where the ferry was docked outside of town. She unhitched her eager horses and began navigating the congested street towards the O'Reilly camp. The whole time she was headed towards camp was spent looking for any indication of the ferry crossing, such as a possible street sign. A crowd was blocking the road, causing her to stop in the middle of the road, caught in thought about the ferry. Suddenly, two obscene men were being hurled out of the door of a saloon. Josie, unfortunately, was right in their path way. She was completely immobilized by traffic. There was no going forward or back. She tried to side-step the horses to avoid the two men as best she could. These men were in the dust right under her horses' feet. Her horses shied to avoid them.

"Watch your horses, you filthy coyote!" a dirty, scarred-faced man yelled at her.

"You can't kick us out. We'll burn the place down," the second man yelled back at the saloon. His hat had fallen off, and Josie could see an awful scare where a large portion of his scalp had been cut away. As he turned around, he looked at Josie with cold gray eyes.

"What are you looking at, little girl?" he snarled while standing up, dusting himself off.

"Mighty fine-looking horses, don't you think Col?" leered the first man.

Josie didn't say anything. She kept her eyes forward began to inch towards camp in the crowded street. The intoxicated men continued to walk beside her horse, speaking loudly.

"Why would a whelp of a girl need two fine horses, and we ain't got none, Ed?" the scare face man said.

"Seems we could take the horses, and no one would know a thing until we were long gone," said Col.

She was scared and kept inching her horses forward in the crowd looking for a break where some distance could be put between these drunks and herself. Josie was trying not to show how truly

terrified she was at the moment. These ruffians were nothing but trouble, and they had their eyes on her. If Josie was a man, these cowards would probably move along; alas, she wasn't. A girl was an easy target to harass or rob. All she had done was be in the wrong spot, at the wrong time.

A burly middle-aged man with blonde curly hair in dirty buckskins sidled his horse next to hers from the confines of the crowded street then spoke, "Howdy, miss, my name is Rocky Pete. I couldn't help but notice these men… are they bothering you?" He had been observing for a few moments while working his horse forward.

"Yes," Josie exclaimed louder than she meant to with big frightened eyes.

Rocky Pete swung off his horse before Josie could blink an eye. The crowd parted in tense anticipation of what was going to happen next. Pete quickly swung a quick, solid right at the man closest to him, knocking him to the ground. The second scoundrel, Col, came around Josie's horse to be sharply kicked in the knee cap by Pete. The blow forced the joint to reverse from its natural angle. The first man, Ed, staggered to his feet when Pete hit him with an upper cut that made his jaw chatter. Rocky Pete's hands were like tempered steel from years of hard physical labor.

Col and Ed were both taller than Pete, but neither had the hard-trained muscles that come with working physically hard in all seasons of weather, year after year. Col ensnared Pete from behind in a bear hug while Ed came at Pete swinging, landing a left haymaker that seemed to have no effect on the granite-like mountain man. Before Ed could throw another punch, Pete squatted down and flung Col over his back into the Ed. Knocking both Ed and Col to the ground like a couple of rag dolls. Col came up like a catamount from the ground. His partner, Ed, was unconscious from hitting his head on a wagon wheel when Col landed on him. "One scoundrel down, one to go," Josie thought to herself as she watched the fight in front of her.

Pete and Col circled each other. Pete timed a solid right to Col's ribs. Col stepped, shifting all his weight to land a left, but his momentum was interrupted by Pete's side stepping. Pete and Col stood toe-to-toe, momentarily exchanging blows. Col losing his patients with his ineffectual blows, charged at his opposition. Pete squatted down as Col charged at him, like a bull, using Col's momentum, throwing him over head against a

wagon in the crowded street. Col hit with a massive thud crumpled to the ground like a discarded rag. He didn't bother to get up.

Rocky Pete stepped back into his saddle and looked at Josie with a grin, his blue eyes twinkling.

"I am sorry you had to see that little miss," Pete said, slightly out of breath.

"Thank you, I was stuck in the middle of the road because of wagon traffic, just trying to figure out where the ferry crossing is located. The next thing I know, I have those two ruffians causing problems. It was just so crowded, I couldn't get away," Josie explained, half flustered at the events that just happened.

"I came into Independence this morning, just sold my hides. I was just fixing to lay in some supplies and head back home to the Rockies. When I see those two side-winders bothering you. I couldn't stand by and let them coyotes bother a young girl like you. Couldn't count myself much of a man if I just didn't help when I spotted your problem. They won't be bothering anyone for a little while, and… I got to have a little fun," half chuckling.

"Don't usually see pretty young ladies out by themselves. Where are your folks? Are you lost or in some sort of trouble?" Pete said with genuine concern.

"My Pa is sick. That is why I had to come to town by myself, to get the supplies we needed and to find out about the ferry?" Once again, she was lying.

"Well, the ferry is outside of town a few miles west. You can't miss it because there is a long line of wagons waiting to go over the river. There is a second ferry that takes livestock and passengers. The second one doesn't have the line that the first does to cross. It is a might faster to load people and stock versus them prairie schooners. Is there anything else I can help you with, young miss?"

"Thank you, Pete. That was the last thing I needed to know before heading back to camp. I really do appreciate your help with those scoundrels. Thanks once again," Josie then turned her horses away from the chaos of Independence.

Josie walked her horses at a steady gait back to camp. It was only mid-morning, but she had enough excitement for a whole day. The sky was a little overcast and threatened rain. She could smell

the heavy humidity in the air. Gratefully she had bought a new rain slicker in town. It was still early enough in the day to saddle the pack animals, get across the river, and find a place to camp for the night. Josie unsaddled upon broaching the O'Reilly wagon, walking her horses into her camp. All was peaceful. Walking over to Ma O'Reilly's, Josie spied Ma holding a little one on her lap, singing softly her red hair was falling out of her bun. She was the epitome of motherhood; it was a beautiful vision.

"Hello, me dearie, did you find your father?" Ma O'Reilly asked with genuine concern.

"Yes, he met up with some old neighbors of ours from back East and is going to meet me at the ferry. Last night he had been visiting in the saloon and didn't realize it had grown dark. He decided to stay in town with our neighbors rather than try to find me in the dark. Pa and Sam, our old neighbor, were always good friends but had not spoken over the winter. Neither knew the other had decided to come West in the spring. Independence is the jumping-off spot to the trail," Josie felt guilty lying to this kind woman. Somehow, she felt Ma knew she was lying to her, but Ma had the grace to not say anything.

"Here, dearie, hold the little one, and I'll make us a nice fresh pot of coffee. Mind the laddie, he has been a wee bit fussy all day, has a bit of a fever…probably just teething… me poor little dear," Ma O'Reilly handed her the child in one quick motion and was making them coffee before she objected. Josie knew that she should be moving on, but a cup of coffee would help her get through the rest of her busy day. Ma O'Reilly brought out a pan of her delightful biscuits to have with their coffee.

"Your Pa puts a lot of responsibility on you lass. Leaving you by yourself and then sending you to get the animals, to be returning, and be meeting him."

"Since Ma died, it has just had to be that way for Pa and me to get by. We each have the things that we do. Where are the other children?" Josie was trying to change the subject.

"Me other boys are with their father doing something with the stock. Them boys are always happy to be following after their father doing this and that. I love me boys wouldn't trade them for the world. But do you think the good Lord in six children would see fit to give me one lass to follow

me around? Must mean I'm meant to have more children," Ma slapped her leg and laughed. Changing tones, she asked, "When did your mother die? You know a daughter is always a mother's pride whether it's here on earth or heaven above."

"My Ma died last fall; she had pneumonia. After she died, that's when Pa and I decided to go West. Ma and Pa always planned to come West. Now we are doing it, just without Ma. This winter was really hard without her. The house was so quiet. I miss talking to her and her cooking. My Ma was an amazing cook."

"It's a hard thing for a girl to lose her mother. I lost me mother, when I was nine and felt that I had to grow up at that moment and fill me mother's shoes. There were many a time that I had questions that I wished I had a mother to ask and get answers. Yes, it tis hard on a girl not having a mother."

They spoke of things that had to be done on the trail, like cooking and laundry items that become a difficult task while on the trail. They chatted for only too short a time before Josie handed Ma O'Reilly the child and said her goodbyes.

Ma O'Reilly was such a warm, loving woman, Josie reflected. In some way, Josie wished she could just travel with the O'Reilly family over the trail. Knowing better deep down inside, she needed to get to Pa as fast as she possibly could. Josie also couldn't risk anyone finding out about her money either. She walked to her little pack train with a bit of reluctance and then loaded them up for the day. The animals were well rest and eager to be on the move. Leading the animals through camp then, Josie gave one last look back and saddled up, following the road towards town once again.

CHAPTER SIX: ALL BOGGED DOWN

A well-rutted wagon trail spurred off the main road leading towards the West. Josie assumed it led to the ferry. She was right. Farther down the trail were several wagon trains waiting to cross the river. On the West side of the river were several other wagon trains that had already crossed on the ferry. A second ferry was shuttling people and animals back and forth. That was the second ferry that Rocky Pete had mentioned to her. She worked her way carefully down into the line for the second ferry and tried to act as if everything was perfectly normal. It wasn't every day that you see a girl leading a pack train. Josie pulled her bonnet up over her head, hiding in the confines of the shelter of her bonnet. Hoping people wouldn't observe how out of place or nervous she was in the line. Her animals were equally nervous, in line with so many other strange animals. The Jennies kept coming up and nuzzling the horses. The whole pack train made blowing noises and stomping, reflecting their distress. Everywhere the air was full of strange sounds from the creaking wagons, men yelling, and animals bawling. Josie's heart was beating in anticipation of trouble. The air was becoming thicker with the feel of impending rain. Her hope was to simply get across the river before it started to rain.

Josie observed the people in front of her crossing, paying close attention to procedure. When it came Josie's turn to board the ferry, she took a deep breath and waited for questions. The questions did not come, to her relief.

"Move forward slowly. It will be sixty cents for each animal and sixty cents for you. That's four dollars and twenty cents," the tired ferry man said flatly, putting his hand out for payment.

She reached in her pouch then handed the man his money. Josie had been diligent in watching what the ferry man charged the passengers ahead of her. He was charging Josie the same amount to cross. The store clerk had told her the truth, things were more expensive on the frontier. Josie and her pack train were halfway across the river when it started to sprinkle. Her new slicker was on the other horse. She would have to wait until they were on the other side of the river to retrieve it. The ferry slowly docked, the pack train disembarked, and others were waiting to board the ferry going East towards Independence. Josie walked her pack train out of the way and retrieved her slicker. By the time she had retrieved her slicker, the rain was picking up speed. She remounted her horse and led her pack train West in the pouring rain, glad to put Independence and its chaos behind her.

***

As Josie undocked, there was an unsavory audience watching her every move.

"Isn't that the girl from town today, Col? Ed asked, pointing across the field.

"I sure think it is. Look at here; she's alone and with more critters."

"It would be ashamed to see such fine animals end up in Indians' hands, don't you think, Col."

"Sure, would be. We better follow along to make sure they stay in white hands."

"We need to get us a couple horses first. Good thing we are surrounded by them…free for the picking," as he said this, he made a sweeping motion at a wagon train remuda.

***

The next four days Josie spent traveling parallel to various wagon trains. It rained non-stop for those days. Josie, even with her slicker on, was wet and cold. Her little pack train was moving along faster than the wagon trains. The wagons were getting bogged down in the mud. Cutting her own trail in the grass, avoiding the extreme mud for the most part, not wholly, but faring a lot better than the wagon trains. Occasionally, the stocks hooves had to be cleaned because they became so caked with mud. When Josie bedded down at night, it was raining. When waking, it was still raining. What made the rain and mud worse was only finding camps that offered minimal shelter. Josie would rustle around the base of bushes and trees to come up with enough dry tinder and sticks to make coffee at night. At least the coffee was there when camp was made at night to cut the chill. All-day long, soaking wet, Josie would think of that hot cup of coffee to keep her going on the trail.

The rain finally ended the sun came out, much to Josie's relief. Finally, warmth from the sun was something that her body forgot existed. No longer were there any wagon trains in view. She began to slowly angle more to the North while still traveling West. Day in and day out, this was her routine, following the green-gray waves of the grass, cutting her own path to the Platte River. Josie was about two weeks out of Independence when she began feeling feverish, had a headache, and her whole body ached.

She continued traveling the rest of the day, feeling ill. The next day it was all she could do to load the animals. Josie climbed into the saddle and vomited. Her perceived need to get a few miles behind her exceeded her concern for her health. The further she traveled, the worst she sweated; her head hurt so bad she could hardly keep her eyes open. Knowing how ill she was, Josie began to search for a place to hole up. Josie didn't know how she stayed in the saddle as long as she did. Her head was swimming, and she was vomiting every few minutes. The pack train and Josie must have traveled fifteen miles before finding the abandoned sod house.

The sod house's roof was collapsed completely; however, it had a well in the side yard. In the back of the house, sheltered by trees and bushes, was an old corral and a trough. The corral was full of long-grown grass. This was what she needed. It took all of Josie's strength to simply unload the animals then put them in the corral. Typically, she cared for her animals by rubbing them down with dry grass at the end of the day. Not today. The pack train could just go roll around in the grass. Josie lay down in the tall plush grass next to the corral. She knew she needed to get the stock water but could do that in a minute. If she could just close her eyes for a few minutes and regain her composure, then she would feel strong enough to get the water.

The next thing Josie was aware of, the Jennies were nuzzling her face through the corral rails. The Jerseys were bawling, and the sky was the pink gray declaring nightfall. Her head felt huge and heavy; her mouth was dry. She stumbled towards the packs grabbed the pail. Somehow, Josie milked the cows even though her hands were swollen, stiff, and sore. She didn't even drink any of the milk. Just the thought of milk made her nauseous. She went to the well, drawing up a couple of buckets of water then, put it in the trough. Luckily some rain water was standing in the trough. She weakly drew up a bucket of water for herself took a deep drink, trying to rid her mouth of the dry pastiness, immediately she vomited. Josie grabbed her bed roll and went to sleep behind the soddy.

The Jerseys were loudly bawling again. She wished she didn't have to get up and milk them. She could wish all she wanted, but it didn't change the reality of the fact: *the cows need milked, and the chickens needed fed.* Begrudgingly Josie stiffly climbed from her bedroll, grabbed the pail then, milked the cows. Added two more buckets of water in the trough and went back to sleep. This was her routine for the next two days: milking cows giving them water, and sleeping. On the third day, she woke feeling a little better. During the cycle of milking and sleeping, her body became covered in red spots that itched. Josie wanted to scratch her skin right off her bones. There had to be something to relieve her misery, an explanation for her illness. Out came the well-worn medical book. Reading through a few different rashes before coming to the one that described hers: chicken pox. The one thing the book said that was of some consolation was once you have the sores with chicken pox, you are past the worst of the illness. "Good thing she was on the mend; they had lost a couple days of travel," she thought. Josie was tired of being ill. She had things to do.

This morning Josie milked the cows, drank some milk, a change from the last few days. The milk did little to satisfy her hunger. All those days of not eating anything finally caught up with her. She was rustling in her pack for the fixings to make some biscuits and some coffee. When in the distance, there were voices. Josie froze in her tracks, not wanting to make any noise that anyone could hear also straining to hear. She heard the voices again but clearer this time. Whoever the voices belonged to, they were getting closer to Josie. Fearful of her safety, she silently walked in a crouched position to her bedroll, where her guns were, and continued to listen.

"Ed, I don't think we are ever going to catch up with that girl with all those animals."

"Shut up, Col! You're not the one walking…so quit your dang- gum complaining."

"Do you think that girl could be over there in that old soddy, Ed? If I was a girl, I'd be looking for a house. You know some place to hole-up."

"No girl is going to stop at some ramshackled busted down soddy. Look, the roof is all caved-in. What good is a house you can't go in? Tell me that, Col. That girl is probably only a little way up the trail yet. If that blasted horse of mine didn't go lame on me in all that mud, we would have already caught her. Next time we steal horses, we steal better ones than the coyote bait we helped ourselves to out of that remuda in Independence."

"When we last seen that girl cross the river, she was traveling in the rain. Wonder if she just kept traveling in the rain and didn't hole up like we did? She could be days ahead of us. Did you think of that, Ed?"

"No darn fool girl would ever travel farther than a place to make camp in that rain, then hole up like we did until it passed over. I can feel it in my bones; she isn't too far from us now. When we do find her, we'll have a whole fancy new rig, and the Indians just killed a little girl," Ed said with a dark chuckle.

Josie heard every word that had been said; she did not doubt the girl they were speaking of was her. She recognized the voices and knew exactly who her followers were. When leaving Independence, she thought of those drunken ruffians far behind her. Come to find out now they were following her out, West was perturbing, to say the least. Josie was grateful that she had not started the coffee or biscuits yet. The aroma of cooking food would have led those despicable men straight to her. Remaining still longer than probably needed, not wanting to make any noise. Eventually, Josie decided that it was safe to continue with cooking. She walked backed to her packs and resumed making biscuits and coffee. While the biscuit was baking in the Dutch oven, she chewed on a piece of jerky. Giving intense thought to the two road agents. It wasn't safe to stay still. Josie would rest here the rest of the day and, itching or not, was getting back on the trail tomorrow.

In the faint yellow light of morning, Josie already had her little pack train on the trail. Feeling a little weak yet much stronger than when she sought refuge at the soddy house. Her pack train seemed glad to be on the move again. They had grown restless in the small confines of the corral. She felt a homey contentment being in the saddle. One of the many things she had discovered on this journey was how clearly a person could look at the world astride a horse. She began noticing things like how

a sound carried or the indentation that remained on the trail from another traveler. She liked to play the game when she saw tracks on the trail of identifying the means of travel, how many people, what type of animals. Then she would make up a story about who they were and where they were headed to. It passed the time.

The other thing about riding a horse was plenty of time to think. Josie found herself reflecting on something learned or heard about the West over the years. All the great adventure stories about Kit Carson and Jim Bridger and many others circle around in her head. Time was also spent reflecting on the many books that Josie had the privilege of reading. Analyzing how they tied to the world right now in 1861. One perspective she studied was the chaos of war because of the impending war over states' rights.

Having read a lot about different wars, it seems in the end, devastation reigns on both sides, the victor and loser. Yet, one side claims victory because their point, want, or need was met. The Neopolic Wars was the perfect example. To continue funding their European campaign, France sold the French holdings that was adjacent to New Orleans. These assets that were sold to the United States were only recently gained from Spain. Yet France having to sell their assets to pursue more war led to the Louisiana Purchase. Neither Spain nor France now had control over the land. They both lost. Without the Neopolic Wars, she would not be heading West into American Territory.

CHAPTER SEVEN: THE WILLOWS

Today Josie found herself thinking about the two villainous men from Independence, Ed and Col. A couple of days ago, learning that these men didn't just intend to rob her but kill her made her hair stand on end. These men didn't belong in society. That is probably why they got thrown out of that saloon in Independence. Josie knew that if the day came when she did run into these men, it was going to be her or them. Thinking that way disturbed her at the core of her being. Yes, she had killed one man because it was survival. This didn't mean there was a desire or want to kill. "Wouldn't it be survival if she encountered this Ed and Col?" she argued with herself. Right now, she was glad to be behind these malicious men, and if she stayed behind them, a deadly encounter with them could be avoided. Josie thought this to be as logical plan that could be formulated. Then pray that this plan will work.

The hypnotic waves of the silver-green grass beckoned onward for the next three days. Josie stopped every evening as dusk was approaching, giving no more thought to Ed and Col. Veering more North than West, adjusting her trail planning to follow the Platte longer… going the Mormon route. She would probably be on a different path than Ed and Col. This thought gave her peace of mind. Josie found herself humming a tune of unknown origins to her pack train and happily moving on down the trail. Enjoying the breeze and the sunshine on her face, happy to be moving forward. Various herds of antelope and one gigantic herd of buffalo had crossed her path. The size of the buffalo herd was unbelievable. When seeing the buffalo, Josie sat her horse and stared in amazement; it was nothing like she had ever seen. Having heard about buffalo herds in her kitchen from visitors from the West, but until you've seen it…words cannot do it justice.

It was about noon when a large stand of willow trees in the middle of her path came into view. Josie had learned growing up that willows only grow where there is water. Not seeing a stream, there was probably a spring there in the middle of the stand. This would be a good spot to let the

animals take a breather and get a little drink of water. As Josie approached the stand of willows, she noticed a campfire that wasn't that old. Well, this would be an excellent place to camp Josie told herself. Getting down from her horse, seeing the grass was flattened. Feeling a slight uneasiness, Josie grabbed her rifle out of the boot off her horse. Something here didn't look right or feel right. Under a far tree, some animal skins looked like they were kicked to the side. When scouting around, she saw blood, a lot of blood, without animal signs. Someone was hurt severely or dead without any doubt in her mind. Josie wanted to leave in case whoever did this came back. Quite candidly, she was scared. Scared or not, if there was a person alive, they needed help.

Taking a deep breath, Josie followed the matted-down grass and blood. She had a feeling that the trail would lead her to the spring, and it did. Next to the spring was an elderly Indian. He had a dark tanned leather complexion, his face full of creases, his hair was almost entirely gray. It was visible even through his shirt the strength that his arms and chest possessed in his youth. He was unconscious. The whole front of his shirt was stained with blood. Standing back and studying

him for a moment for any other wounds, she saw a knife slash across his neck that was caked with blood and hair. Reaching down, Josie, frightened, touched his chest... he was alive.

As much as Josie had wanted to leave this place earlier, that was not happening now. She could not in good conscious leave a wounded person. Taking the chance that whoever done this has gone down the trail was all that could be done at this point. Josie brought her pack train down close to the spring, picketing them on the good grass. She then hurried about making a fire. Rolling out the extra bedroll dragging the old man onto the sougam as carefully as possible. Josie was grateful for all the hard work on the farm, making her more robust than the average girl of thirteen, thankfully giving her the strength to move the old man. Now that the man was away from the spring, she could put some water on to get hot to clean his wounds.

Carefully Josie removed the old man's shirt. The blood had coagulated on his shirt as it was removed; it restarted the bleeding. The old man did not stir during this process. He must have lost a sight of blood. Right away, the large bullet wound in his side was visible. Josie was wholly perplexed about how to treat this wound. She was frightened

to inflict any more pain on the old man than he had already suffered. Going into her pack, she retrieved her medical supplies, soap, and sewing kit. Josie began walking back to the injured old man but abruptly turned back to her bags and retrieved her medical book. The water was hot. She shaved a little soap into the water. Mama always said to use hot soapy water to get something clean. This blood-caked mess definitely needed to be cleaned. She took a handkerchief from her medical supplies and began gently bathing the wounds. Cleaning all the blood away would allow her to see how terrible the injuries really were and enable her to assess how to treat them.

She remembered how to treat the knife cut because Ma had tended a boatman with a nasty deep cut. Since that is what Josie knew how to fix, that it is where she would begin on the old man. Plucking a hair from one of her horse's tails, she then threaded the hair on a needle from her sewing kit. Dipping the hair in the hot water then smoothing the water off the thread between her pinched fingers. This was so the hair was sleek and would glide easier while sewing. She hesitated a moment, having never sewn up a person. Rolling the old man's neck to the side, exposing the slash, allowing the wound to be stitched. The wound was deep. It was amazing it had not bled worse. He was lucky. She stuck the needle into his flesh, drawing the gash closed. Josie continued sewing in neat even stitches until the wound was sealed. "It had been like sewing rabbit hide," Josie reflected.

Now there was the bullet wound to contend with as quickly as possible because it still was bleeding. Knowing where the surgery section of her medical book was, Josie quickly thumbed through it, searching for bullet wounds. When Josie found bullet wounds in the book, she was downright disgusted, to say the least. There were two very brief paragraphs on what to do. The summary of what the book said was: *If the bullet went all the way through- stop the bleeding. If the bullet did not go all the way through-remove the bullet and stop the bleeding.* Rolling the old man over gingerly, the bullet didn't go all the way through. The bullet was going to have to be removed. "Now, how in God's green earth am I going to do that?" she muttered to herself. Josie had never seen anyone remove a bullet. Once, she had dug a few slugs out of a tree to see if two shots were in the same spot. Digging in a tree is quite a bit different.

Namingly, it didn't bleed. Josie had no choice; the bullet wound needed attention. She would have to try her best, despite the poor instructions from her medical book.

Josie had never been squeamish about blood. She was a hunter. What she was squeamish about was: causing pain or death. Sticking the tip of her index finger into the wound, the old man wince. She stuck her finger in deeper to the knuckle that meets her hand. A combination of blood clots and fresh blood oozed up around her finger. She could smell the sweet metallic scent of blood. Sweat was rolling down her forehead. Searching around with her finger, she found the ball. Using her finger, she carefully dislodged the ball from its resting place. "How in tarnation am I going to get that ball out?" she questioned herself. Josie regrettably realized that she would have to cut the wound a little wider then. She could then reach in and grab the ball. Josie hated the idea of making the wound larger but could think of no other way to extract the ball. Taking her razor-sharp Bowie knife, she sliced the skin adjacent to the bullet wound. Blood was gushing everywhere. Forcing the gaping injury open wide while pressing down with the same hand, she could not see the bullet. Josie then, with

her other hand, placed two fingers into the gaping wound, feeling delicately. She worked her fingers like they were tongs, eventually extracting the bullet. Josie began to wash the wound and her hands. She dumped out the old water then put on fresh water to get hot to rewash everything. The water that she had been using had turned into a red slurry. It wasn't going to clean anything at that point. Once everything was cleaned, she bandaged the wounds.

As Josie was caring for her patient, she accepted that she was going to be delayed here for a couple of days at least. She did the sensible thing as the old Indian rested and went about setting up a long-term camp. "When you have stock, the first rule is to take care of them well, and they will take care of you," Josie recited what her father said hundreds of times in her lifetime. She first built a rope corral for her stock, so they had some range of motion. Next, to care for her patient, Josie made a lean-to out of canvas over the old man. She set about to collect firewood and noticed a few rabbit runs. She took advantage of being stationary for a few days by setting a few snares.

Once the camp was set, she lastly decided to make a feast. Josie made some biscuits in her Dutch oven, a pot of stew using jerky and dried vegetables, and of course, coffee. Josie was grateful to have coffee, especially after today's events. She could use a break and a good meal. She was still a little weak from the chicken pox. When the old man woke, he would need some stew. Upon glancing over at the old man, she noticed he was sweating profusely. Touching the old man's head, it was impossible not to notice the fever. Quickly dipping a handkerchief into the cool spring, she placed it on his head. Then she began collecting willow branches. Thankfully they were plentiful to make tea out of later. The tea would help with the old man's fever and pain if he lived long enough to drink any.

The old man didn't wake until the next day. Josie slept lightly, concerned that he would die in the night or whoever did this to him may come back. When he did wake, he didn't speak. The old man just stared at Josie with curious dark eyes while she fed him a few bites of stew. He thirstily drank the offered willow bark tea. When he had his fill, he went back to sleep immediately. He awoke again later in the day; Josie followed the same routine as earlier, once again, the old man resumed his sleep. The old man still was burning a fever.

Not knowing his name and out of respect for his age, Josie began affectionately calling him "Grandfather" to encourage him to eat or drink.

Desperately Josie wanted Grandfather to get well. Grandfather's wounds were healing slowly. They did look better every day. The pack train had been delayed at the willow camp with Grandfather for five days. It would be ideal to stay put so Grandfather could rest. Josie had to make a hard decision not only for Grandfather but for herself. She decided they needed to keep going or their supplies would give out before Fort Laramie, especially since there now was an extra mouth to feed, Grandfather. Grandfather would have to come with her until he was well enough to return to his own people.

Josie had already retrieved the skins from under the trees that were seen on arriving at the willows; she would put them to use. Cutting two fourteen-foot trees down and removing all the branches was the start of building a travois. One of her dad's friends who had gone to the West explained how the Indians traveled all over the plains using travois on their horses. He even explained how they made smaller travois for their dogs. Her Pa's friend had stayed with them for several days.

During that time, he made her a little travois for her dog. Josie paused from her work as she reflected back on the happy memory. She had played with that little travois non-stop. That travois was used to doing her chores and hauling her rag doll. "I wonder what ever happened to my little travois?" she said to herself.

Nonetheless, it was time to build a travois for Grandfather. Good thing she stood there watching every step of that little travois being constructed. Now Josie needed to recreate what she learned on a larger scale and hope and pray she could remember all the process. "I can do this, it may take me more time than a skilled person, but I can build a travois," she said aloud, boosting her confidence. It took Josie almost the whole day to fabricate the latter structure of the travois. She would have to stop and measure to ensure it would fit on the horse securely. She also needed to ensure that it would hold the proper weight. Josie was pleased with her day's work. That night while feeding Grandfather, she explained that tomorrow they would leave there.

He still didn't say anything; however, he smiled.

CHAPTER EIGHT: THE GROWING TRAIN

Before the yellow of morning even touched the sky, Josie was busy breaking camp and loading the little pack train. Josie lined the travois with the extra skins then drug the bedroll onto the travois, tying Grandfather securely in place. She filled all the canteens in case they had to make a dry camp tonight. Lastly, she kicked the dirt over the dying coals of the fire. Josie wasn't sure how far they could travel in a day pulling a travois. What she did know was: every mile was getting them closer to Fort Laramie and to her Pa.

The pack train had grown with the addition of the travois, but they were moving forwards. The grass was still green, and there was a pleasant warm breeze. After about a mile of travel, Josie stepped

down from the saddle, checked, and adjusted the lashings on the travois. Everything was holding securely, and Grandfather was sleeping soundly. The thick prairie grass allowed the travois to be pulled smoother than she had anticipated. Climbing back into the saddle, they continued forward. Josie's stock was in sound shape. She had been traveling slow and steady. With the two unexpected stops, this had given the stock plenty of time to rest. The chickens had even surprised her with a couple of eggs throughout the stay at the willows. She used her bounty to make dumplings, a nice change from biscuits and flap-jacks.

The fields had periodically been plowed in patchwork squares that indicate farming for the last few miles. Adjacent to the patchwork fields were various homes: soddies, cabins, dug-outs. She even spied one lone clapboard home. Josie plodded forward, reading the signs that civilization was closer with every step. Geographically she knew she must be coming to one of the settlements along the Platte River. This meant that she was further down the trail than she initially thought. It was nearing noon when Josie saw a military installment. She didn't know of any military installments on this end Platte; she assumed that it

was Fort Kearny. Somewhere between the rain and the sickness, Josie under-estimated her miles traveled. Joyfully, it dawned on her that would also mean: they were not as far from Fort Laramie as initially thought.

Josie wasn't going to get excited. There was still a chance that she was a long-ways from Fort Kearney. Outside the presumed fort perimeters, a wagon train stopped, and several soldiers talked to the wagon travelers. Josie did not want to stop or take on any supplies because this could draw questions about Grandfather. Josie quickly reminded herself that she didn't have an adult traveling with her; she was in as much danger as Grandfather. The consequences would be worse for Grandfather if things went astray. Josie was all too aware of how whites perceived Indians; she thought it sensible to avoid contact with people.

Josie did, however, need to speak to someone to find out where they were at along the Platte. She needed to confirm that this was Fort Kearney. The closer to the fort, her heart raced, and her mind was buzzing hive looking for a way to get the information Josie needed without drawing attention to her pack train. When she was closer to the fort, Josie resolved that the best solution was:

to speak to one of the women on the wagon train. Talking to herself, Josie began to justify her decision, "Back in Independence, Ma O'Reilly had been kind and helpful maybe, another woman would be helpful." The closer to the fort with the pack train, the smell of the mingled aroma of various cooking fires, animals, and the Platte River hit the senses. These smells were comforting to Josie, bringing up memories of a different time when she was back home along the river. This time last year, she was home with Ma. They were cooking and enjoying the fresh smell of the Mississippi River. Josie sighed contently then; she brought her attention to the matter at hand: observing the women to figure out which one to ask for information.

Working the pack train closer to the wagon train, Josie observed the trail broke families utilizing the break. The women were taking advantage of the stop to wash laundry, make soap, to do baking, and do a dozen other chores that they had got behind on the trail. Children were helping with various tasks or playing, enjoying a break from the rigors of the trail. Men were busy visiting, trading, and doing multiple repairs to the wagons and equipment, preparing for the long journey ahead of

them. Josie was studying the wagon train people casually, not wanting to draw attention to herself. Half hopingly, she longed to see the O'Reilly wagon; she knew it was a long shot. If she did see Ma O'Reilly, it would reduce her risk of problems. Josie could hear her inner voice reminding her, "That to speak to people was a great danger not only to herself but to Grandfather." She had to dismiss her inner voice because it didn't change the fact: she needed information.

Josie sat in her saddle tall, trying to appear confident while walking her pack train parallel to the adjacent wagon train. She watched and gauged the people's responses to her and her pack train. Most people were so engrossed in their own tasks they didn't so much as acknowledge that they were passing. Others quickly looked away. It was if they engaged in a conversation or interaction with a person, not from their wagon train, their world would crumble. Josie finally passed a friendly man who smiled and lifted his hand in a wave. She had not prepared herself to speak to a man. Josie had been sure it was going to be a woman who would reach out that she found herself lost for words momentarily. Man or woman, the knowledge would be the same. She would approach this man.

The man was tall and lanky with a shock of stick-straight dark brown hair hanging in his face. He was busy fixing a shoe on his horse. Josie dismounted then left her pack train where it was standing. The horses were ground-hitched. This would keep her pack train waiting for a moment or two while she walked over to the man. Josie suddenly became concerned that she was brazen to speak to an unknown man without negative social backlash; however, she needed information, and he looked to be her best source. "Things are different in the West," Josie mentally chided herself at being worried about foolish social ideals. She laughed to herself, thinking, "Before long, I will be worried about fashion, being fashionable."

Josie timidly approached the man then asked, "Excuse me, sir…Could you help me, please?"

"I'll help if I can miss," he said, putting down the horse's leg then, pushing his wayward hair out of his face.

"I need to know what settlement this is? We are on our way to Fort Laramie."

"This must be your first time over the trail. Well, this isn't Fort Laramie; it's Fort Kearny. Doesn't look like much of a fort, neither does Fort

Laramie. I remember thinking that forts had to have big stockades around them. Not out here on the great American Desert."

"Yes, this is the first time across the trail, and somehow we got confused on our location. Thank you for the information, sir. Before I go, can you tell me anything about the trail up head to Fort Laramie?"

"Just follow the river. Watch for the Arapaho and Sioux. They're warring with the whites. Things have been quiet, but you never know when that will change. The next place you'll come up to is Fort Bernard. Then eight miles further West is Fort Laramie."

"Thank you for the help, sir," Josie said, then waved and walked backed to her pack train.

Before un-hitching the horses, she checked the travois. It was still secure. She then gave Grandfather a long patient drink of water from the canteen. Josie felt a calmness come over her. They were closer to Pa than she thought they were this morning. The concerns about provisions and travel time seeped away with every sip from the canteen. Then, she picked up her lines, remounted her horse, and continued West.

***

If Josie had gone into the Fort Kearney, her experience at the fort wouldn't have been so pleasant. She would have seen Ed and Col. Those two road agents did not see Josie because they were too caught up spending the last of their ill-gotten money drinking themselves into a stupor. Josie no longer gave any thought to Ed and Col. She was figuring that she was miles behind them because of the delay at the willows with Grandfather. Even in his drunkenness, Ed could not let the idea of his new obsession go.

"Col, was in tarnation did she go?" Ed slurred.

"She went to get us another bottle."

"Not, that girl! I am talking about that dang blasted girl with all my fine-looking critters. I walked halfway from Independence to here for those critters, and they're mine."

"Ed, we got us a herd of critters due to peoples 'generosity.' We don't need no more critters. What you and me need is more whiskey!"

"I decided they were my critters, so…they are going to be my critters."

CHAPTER NINE: APPEARANCES

The pack train had uneventfully made their way three days west of Fort Kearny. The day was pleasantly warm, showing just a glimpse of the sweltering heat of summer that was right around the corner; the rhythmic swaying movement of the horse was peacefully lulling Josie to sleep. She had been half dozing in the saddle oblivious of the world when suddenly she came over a rise to find herself abruptly forced wide awake, flanked by several braves on horseback. Quickly assessing the change in circumstances, she knew that it was futile to run from them or fight them. The only logical option was to remain still. She took a deep breath and silently raised a string of fervent prays that these were peaceful people. Looking at the

menacing glares, Josie instinctually doubted if these braves were peaceful.

One of the younger braves from the group sidled his black-spotted horse close to the travois. His eyes were assessing locked with Josie's. This particular brave carried a long-decorated lancet that he hoovered over Grandfather. Josie did not advert her eyes; she maintained a trained locked stare. The brave then made a downward motion that looked as though he was going to strike Grandfather with his weapon.

"Stop! Grandfather is hurt," Josie cried out in Sioux. The young brave stopped mid-motion in what was to be a killing strike. He was startled and confused that a white girl was speaking Sioux.

Josie's words caused a hum of conversation among the braves in a language Josie did not know. There was no question in her mind that this impromptu conversation was about her and her pack train. Josie's mind was assessing the situation moment by moment. The more time that went by, the more she realized that they were in grave danger. Josie was grateful that the brave had stopped his intended action when she spoke. She didn't know why her words worked but was grateful

nonetheless. "Why question something when it works…just be grateful," she thought. What was going to happen next, God only knew. She reminded herself to take a deep breath. Remembering what her Ma said about inner strength, Josie knew that she must pull from that well deep within herself at this moment, staying composed and brave.

"The strange girl spoke Sioux. We are at peace with the Sioux. I do not want to cause a war with them," one brave voiced firmly with a look of worry clouding his expression.

"This girl is nothing… white and evil. She can speak Sioux. That does not make her Sioux. The whites are here to destroy us as a people. One less white, one less problem. We should just kill them then, go home to our people." When this young brave spoke these words, two of the other very young braves agreed. The youngest braves' solution was always to kill and to cause war. They were young and had not lived through the hardship and struggles that war caused. All they think of is glory, not the consequences of the war: the loss of life, home, family, horse, property.

"I think she is a Sioux medicine woman. She has trained her cows to carry birds, and her long ear horses follow with no ropes. This girl did not show any fear in our presents. Her medicine is strong. We should leave her to go on her way and not disturb the spirits because we are foolish." His words were met by agreement by the older warriors. These warriors had gained enough years in this world to start to have a more immense respect and more profound knowledge of the spirit world that can only be obtained through prayer and age. It is a rite of passage caused by experience that the younger braves could not understand yet.

The Warrior Chief, Red Feather, spoke, quieting the band of braves, "This girl and her grandfather's fate is not our decision to make. She is not clearly white, nor clearly Sioux. She is a mix of both. The council will decide if she is more human-like us…or white. For now, we will take them back to camp as prisoners," then looking at the young braves said, "and unharmed." Warring had brought him great influence and honor in the tribe. Red Feather knew that his words carried significant influence because he was such a victorious warrior leading many war parties over the years. He has found that as he transitions into a Gray-hair that he

would much rather have peace. His job was to teach the young braves, guiding them on their journey as warriors.

The young braves needed to learn to make wise choices for the tribe in matters of war. There is a time to battle and a time to retreat to fight another day. If braves are lost in battle, who will provide meat for his tipi? A good warrior knows that his brother will provide meat for his tipi, but does he think beyond to his brother dying also. If too many braves die, there is no one to protect the village and provide meat. Being a good leader was about looking at the larger impact of the action. Someday, the young would think about these things, but today they are young and only think of counting coupe.

Still, Red Feather needed to deal directly with the prisoners. This was part of his role as leader.

Red Feather spoke devoid of any facial expression, "We are taking you to our village as our prisoner. Do not try to escape, or we will kill you. Follow us."These words were spoken in Sioux while looking Josie challengingly in the eyes as an act of deliberate aggression.

Josie nodded her head downward in slow consent then, followed beleaguering. It wasn't as if there was much choice but to follow, see as she was surrounded by braves. At this moment, Josie knew the situation was beyond her control. Asher pack train was being led forward to this foreign camp. Her mind was flooded with thoughts. "I should have been paying better attention instead of dozing in the saddle." "What could she have done even wide awake?" she reminded herself. No matter if she was awake or asleep, the scenario of running into the braves was beyond bad. They could have killed them right then and there. "No matter how tranquil things seem in the West, the danger is always present, and the second you forget that you are dead," Josie noted for the future. Even if you know danger is present, you could still be dead. Josie chastises herself for her lack of caution all the way to the Indian camp. During herself beratement, Josie did note her surroundings carefully in case the opportunity to escape arose. She wouldn't be disoriented. She still couldn't shake the feeling that if she had been attentive, things would have worked out differently. Deep in her heart, she thought this drama was probably unavoidable though logically, she knew better.

The braves camp was only a short distance from where they had found Josie and Grandfather. There was twenty tipi's that she counted as they approached the camp. The closer they drew brought a greeting of dogs and dirty children coming to observe the procession of braves and her pack train. The women stopped their work to stare as the pack train passed. Josie could feel the heat rise on her face in embarrassment. This was one of the moments in her life she wished she had her bonnet on to hide the flush from her face. To put her bonnet on now would be to show her weakness…fear. She absolutely refused to reveal how scared she was to anyone, especially her captors. Josie and her pack train were forcefully led to a place next to a tipi at the edge of camp. All the braves filed away, except for one.

"You will stay here. If you try to leave… you will be killed," Red Feather said resolutely in Sioux.

Josie replied without a hint of pleading in her voice, "I need to leave to go to my father. He waits for me." Josie was cautious not to sound pleading or weak. Weakness would not be respected.

"You will stay here with Two Rabbits until the council has decided what is to be done with you

and your grandfather," Red Feather then turned his horse abruptly then walked away.

At the mention of Two Rabbits, an elderly woman with beautiful white hair parted in the middle tied in two long pony tails ornamented with tuffs of rabbit fur with bead work and sparkling brown eyes came through the tipi door, looked at Josie, and smiled. She was missing a few teeth; this didn't interfere with the beauty of her incredible big heartfelt smile. The smile had a calming effect. She stepped gracefully from her door. The color of her buck skin dress with the color of her skin created the image of a deer stepping out of the woods into the meadow. Her whole aura was tranquil. Her face showed some of her age, mainly in the deep laughter lines around her eyes.

"Come, little one, make your camp next to mine," Two Rabbits said in Sioux. Two Rabbits had heard Red Feather speak to this girl, and her curiosity was peaked when she listened to the first Sioux word be spoken.

Josie was perplexed as to what tribe this camp belonged to, "Is this a Sioux village?"

"No, little one, this is an Arapaho village. The Arapaho are friends of the Sioux people. I am also Sioux."

"If the Arapahoe are friends with the Sioux, then there must be a mistake because I am Sioux and should not be a prisoner. You are Sioux? You live with the Arapaho people yet are not their prisoner."

"Once your camp is made, then, I may tell you my story, little one of how I came to belong here among the Arapahoe," Two Rabbits then went inside her tipi as gracefully as she came outside.

Josie just stood in frozen shock for a moment processing the events that had transpired. "Why hadn't her captors taken her animals or weapons?" Josie pondered. Red Feather must have felt his warning sufficient to prevent Josie from doing anything foolish: *to leave would be to die*. Fifteen feet away from Two Rabbits tipi was a stand of cotton wood trees. Camp could be made there. She hoped that the Arapaho did not consider the trees too far away from Two Rabbits' supervision, but they needed the shelter of the trees to set a proper camp. First thing first, before Josie did anything to make camp, she needed to check on Grandfather.

"Grandfather here drink some water. Things are looking grim right now, but we will get through this," Josie said, smiling down. "Just drink some water, Grandfather."

Grandfather's eyes opened slowly. They were gazing into Josie's eyes. His forehead wrinkled as his eyebrows raised in an expression of deep concern.

"Granddaughter, it will be fine. You are a good girl," he said in a soft clear raspy voice. Those were the first words that Grandfather had ever spoken to Josie, and they were in English. He then closed his eyes slowly then quickly returned to sleep.

Grandfather spoke to her at last, which meant he was starting to recover at last. Happiness flooded over her for a moment. She had been doing everything she could to help Grandfather and has worried over his recovery non-stop. Josie took a deep breath to calm herself. Grandfather was not well yet. She shouldn't get ahead of herself. She still needed to get Grandfather and her out of this Arapaho camp, then to Fort Laramie, where Pa was. Once they got to Pa, things would be easier. Pa always seemed to know how to handle every

situation or problem. He would square his shoulders, fix his eyes on the problem, take a deep breath, then use logic to break the issue apart. Pa always said, "The biggest projects start with the first action then is completed by a series of smaller actions." Josie needed to start with an action. Before she could do that, she would have to be brave like her Ma and push her fear way down deep into the recesses of her soul. Josie reminded herself no one respects weakness. If they were to survive, she would need to command respect. This was the first action in solving this problem, at least if Josie was looking at things through Pa's eyes. This was scary; how was she going to command respect?

Josie unloaded the pack train. Using the trees and ropes to make a make-shift corral for her animals. Taking her time rubbing each of them down with grass. As soon as the chicken cages were set down on the ground, the chickens were happily catching bugs. She built a quick lean-to out of some branches and the canvas from her pack. The grass was quickly cut to make a bed then Grandfather was placed under the lean-to on his bedroll. She stored saddles and packed goods near the lean-to for convenience. Josie then set about collecting

firewood. There was only a little firewood, mostly small twigs. On scouting the hillside, she found some buffalo droppings. In that Lansford Hastings *Emigrants Guide to the Oregon and California Trail,* the book Josie read before leaving, buffalo chips could be used in place of firewood. Willing to give it a try, she filled her skirt full of the dry droppings.

When returning to camp, Josie took her pail down to the river them filled it with the murky Platte River water. Getting water was not a simple thing when along the Platte. The water had a large amount of silt. The pail of water would have to sit undisturbed, allowing the mud to settle to the bottom. By dinner time, she would be able to fill the canteens from the pail straining off the sludge from the bottom. Josie would get a bucket of water at night to have usable water by morning. Josie returning to camp filled the coffee pot from the canteen then made some coffee. In a pot off to the side, add some water to boil to make Grandfather some willow bark tea.

No matter what angle Josie studied the situation, it looked like she and Grandfather would be here for a while, at least the remainder of the day. Josie could sit there and stew about their problematic

position or make the best of it. Choosing to make the best of the situation, she pulled out her Dutch oven and made some biscuits. In another pot, she made a stew using some of her dried vegetables, wild onions she found yesterday, and shaved jerky. While the food was cooking, Josie made an assessment of their provisions. They had enough supplies for an easy three weeks. She calculated that they were only about ten days from Fort Laramie…but what kind of delay was this going to be? Or were their captors just going to kill them? She wasn't going to allow herself to think that way.

Josie needed to remain busy so that her courage wouldn't wain. Keeping busy had always been her salvation when things were difficult in life. It helped her funnel her emotions into a task. What she needed now was a chore of some sort to fill her hands and mind. She knew what she could. When Josie had found Grandfather, his moccasins were walked almost entirely through. He desperately needed a new pair. Josie had thought about making him a pair when they were at the spring with the willows; she decided against it because he may not live. Now things have changed. Grandfather spoke, and he called her Granddaughter. No one had ever

called her granddaughter before. Both sets of grandparents had passed away before she was ever born. It would have been nice to have grandparents. She had heard so many tales about her grandparents she felt as if she knew them.

No sense thinking about what would never be. It was time to make Grandfather's moccasins. He would be strong and well and need them before long. Taking one of the old skins found with Grandfather, Josie marked out Grandfather's old moccasins. Then cut them with her Bowie knife and sewed them up with sinew. She did this just the way her Ma had taught her. Josie, busy in task, thought that my Ma learned this from her Ma, my grandma. The things my Ma and Pa taught me are part of their Ma and Pa. "I am my grandparents in action," Josie said aloud as she pondered this thought deeper.

***

Key tribal members watched everything that Josie, Long Ears, was doing, trying to discern who this girl was. If she was Sioux, she was an odd Sioux. If she was white, she was an odd white. This girl was doing the things that demonstrated what a good Indian woman did, reflecting she was properly trained by the women in her family. She had made a good camp. She was caring for the old man. She was making moccasins. These were things expected of the women of the Arapaho and of the Sioux. It was mesmerizing how she had some magic on her cows to carry birds in cages. Never seen cows carry anything, let alone caged birds. The long-eared horses follow without a rope because of her great medicine. She is little more than a child yet acts like a woman. Long Ears showed the courage of a brave speaking up in defense of her Grandfather. All these little pieces would be taken into consideration when the council decided Josie's fate. Their observation of Josie would continue until the council meeting. As for the old man, Long Ears' grandfather, his fate was tied to hers.

***

The food was done cooking at Josie's camp. The scent had been tantalizing a hungry Josie the whole time it was cooking. Glancing up at the tipi a few feet away, Josie thought of Two Rabbits by herself. She knew that Two Rabbits had to be smelling the food too. There was more than enough food for the three of them, Josie thought while tipping her head to the side. Two Rabbits

didn't even have a cooking fire going. Josie had eaten many cold meals on the trail and knew how precious a hot meal was to a person. Determined to share, she then walked to Two Rabbits' tipi calling out.

"Two Rabbits, Two Rabbits…"

"Yes, little one, what do you need?" she said, coming out of her tipi.

"Please come to our camp and eat. We have plenty."

"Let me get my dish," she then went back inside her tipi.

Two Rabbits was smiling with her whole face when she emerged from her tipi seconds later. Josie served Two Rabbits some stew and a biscuit at the fire then fed Grandfather his stew. Two Rabbits was quiet while she ate. Josie poured Grandfather some willow branch tea. Noticing the arthritic hands of Two Rabbits, she also poured her a cup of tea. Josie was hungry but would not eat until Grandfather and Two Rabbits had been cared for, then it would be her turn. It was only respectful for her to wait: feeding the sick and the guest first. Two Rabbits was done eating and had

washed her dish with some sand. Grandfather had finished his dinner and was once again sleeping again.

"Eat, little one," we are fine Two Rabbits said, motioning towards the kettle with her aged hands.

"I am hungry. I like to make sure that Grandfather eats so that he will get well," Josie was filling her plate while she was speaking.

"What was that you gave your grandfather and me to drink?"

Swallowing a mouthful of food before answering, "It was willow bark tea. It is good for healing and for pain. I have been making it for Grandfather while he is getting well. When I looked over, I noticed your hands look painful, so I gave you some tea, thinking it might help." She shoveled another spoonful of stew into her mouth as she finished speaking.

"That was kind of you to notice my hands. There are many great wonders that a person sees at my age, leaving the spirit just as young as always. The body does not stay as young," Two Rabbits looks at her aged arthritic hands. Then remembering there was something more, she wanted to say, "I

thought that it was willow bark tea, but was not sure."

"Two Rabbits, if you are Sioux, how did you come to live among the Arapaho?" Josie asked while tearing a piece of biscuit to sop up the gravy from her stew.

"That was a long time ago when I was twenty seasons. It was in the time right before the Cheyenne, Sioux, and Arapahoe made an alliance to drive out the Comanche. My family had been killed in a raid by the Cheyenne. I was not there when the raid happened. I had been collecting herbs. When I realized that all my people were dead decided to go back North to the rest of my people. I was halfway home when I was found by a spring. A brave, Many Horses, found me then took me back to his camp. I came to the Arapaho people at first as a prisoner. I eventually, many years later, became Many Horses bride. This is not common for an outsider to marry into the Arapaho. Usually, the man goes to live with the woman's family when they are married in the Arapaho tradition. Family is everything.

Many Horses was good to me even as his prisoner. He would not allow the other women to

abuse me like they did other women, prisoners. Many Horses was a widow and had a tiny baby. His wife had died in childbearing. As his prisoner, it was my job to care for his child and tipi. I had been his prisoner for three years when the alliance had been formed between our people. By the terms of the alliance, I was free to return to my people. Many Horses asked me to stay and be his wife. I wasn't sure at first because I wanted to return to my people. I had grown to love him and the child that I had mothered all this time. I had made friends among the women. Many Horses was an important man. My band of Sioux had long been dead. I chose to stay and have been Arapaho since.

Now I am old. Many Horses has been gone for many seasons. I am an old woman alone," Two Rabbits said these final words while taking a drink from her cup. Josie refilled the cup wanting the old woman to stay and visit.

"Where are your children, Two Rabbits?" Josie asked curiously.

"I had four handsome, strong, brave sons. They grew into great warriors like their handsome father. They went on many raids, counted coupe, and had many horses each. There comes a time when your children grow and leave your tipi. That is what you want for them, to each have such success to support a family. They each found wives in different bands of Arapaho's. As is the tradition, they went to live with their wife's family. I believe they are well. It would have been nice if one would have found love in this band…but they did not. We travel once a year to meet all the bands at a gathering. I see them some years. They are busy with their own families now."

"What of you, little one? Where is your family?"

"My mother is dead. My father is in Fort Laramie. I have traveled a long way by myself to get to my father. My father does not know that my mother is dead. I had a little sister who died of a fever when I was small. I can remember my little sister only a small bit. Mother said we weren't even two years apart in age."

"You have your grandfather, little one at least with you, little one?"

"He is not my grandfather. I was traveling to my father when I found him. He had been attacked and left for dead. I mended his wounds the best I could and have been taking care of him since. Hoping he can get well. I didn't know his name. Out of

respect for his age, I began calling him Grandfather," Josie said while giving Grandfather a side-long look.

"You could have just left him to die; many would have."

"I could not leave him to die. I could see he was once a fine brave. He deserves respect. He deserves to live out his days with sunlight on his face and a breeze through his hair."

"You see a lot for such a young one... Your eyes are the color of the sky. I have not known a Sioux with your eye color. You speak Sioux well, was your mother, Sioux?"

"Yes, my mother was Sioux. Often when it was just us, we would speak Sioux at home. I speak English most of the time. I can speak some French because we traded with some Frenchman. My mother could speak French fluently because of the missionaries. It is necessary to speak multiple languages to trade and learn things. Of course, you speak Sioux and Arapaho but do you speak any other languages?" Josie suspected that she spoke English because Two Rabbits recognized the word grandfather.

"I speak English and French because of traders when I was a child. You are right, little one; it is necessary to speak many languages. Language has always been easy for me. I quickly learned it and was able to help the people of my village. We also had passing missionaries before we were at war with the white man. I would speak with them. I am glad I learned the language quickly because I first came to the Arapaho as a prisoner. I didn't speak any Arapahoe and needed to learn very quickly. That was a scary time in my life being prisoner and not understanding the words that were being spoken."

"Two Rabbits, you mention war as if it is nothing. You use war to mark your memory of events. You remember before one war and after another. Just now, you spoke of a time before the Sioux were at war with the white man. The world is insane! Arapaho are at war with the whites. The whites are at war with themselves. I hate war. I left my home in the East to come here to be with my father because of war. Why can't people sit down and come to agreements? There is always one war or another. Don't people get tired of fighting?" Josie said in a huff of anger.

"Little one, it is not that easy to get tired of war. People lie...things change...the world changes. People don't know how to accept change that has happened, so they fight, or they don't want change, so they fight. People make deals and change their minds, then they fight. People have war to gain glory or property, so they fight. It has always been so. To some people, war is about power. War is the way of life," Two Rabbits tried to explain.

"I just want to live in peace. I don't want to fight anyone," Josie sighed.

"This I understand, little one. I am old and tired. I no longer want war. I also want to live in peace. Sometimes in order to protect my peace, I must fight or war. Life is not always as simple as we would like it to be."

"I look forward to getting to Fort Laramie and being with my father. There we will have a life of peace. Grandfather, if he wants to stay, he can. We will be a family. We will work to live with the land and be happy. We will be far away from all this warring... I need to get there soon enough that I can prepare for winter. My father will be only preparing for himself. Now there will be Grandfather and me. Two more people to plan for

provisional needs. I don't know what supplies we can get at Fort Laramie. I know I will need to do a lot of hunting. We will need the meat and the hides."

"You are a hunter, little one?" Two Rabbits was surprised.

"Yes, I have been hunting for years. My father was often away. It was my responsibility to bring home fresh meat. I also set snares to get rabbits. We would use the meat to eat fresh or smoke or jerk. The hides were needed to make moccasins and clothes and to trade. It was important that I learned to hunt. Besides, I absolutely enjoy hunting. The quiet of the hunt. Then the joy of a successful hunt is exhilarating."

"That is traditionally a braves job. Women don't hunt. We butcher the meat and prepare it. We take care of the hides. We make the clothes and the moccasins, but we don't hunt. I find you interesting little one…." Two Rabbits was smiling at Josie.

"My mother made sure that I could do the traditional woman things also like cook and sew. My parents thought it was important for me to think for myself and be able to do for myself. They

were always trying to impart a lesson from a book or activity. I liked being independent. My parent didn't have to tell me to do my chores. I knew what needed to be done and did it. I wish my parents were here right now to teach me a lesson about being in an Arapaho camp rather than on the trail to Fort Laramie."

"Remember the lessons that your parents taught you, and things will be fine."

"What is going to happen to Grandfather and me?" Josie asked somberly.

"That I don't have the answer to. The only reason the braves didn't kill you right away was you were a young Indian girl alone with a travois. They couldn't tell if you were Arapaho or not. You have Indian hair and skin. Then when they approached, they saw your blue eyes and decided to kill you. Then you spoke out in Sioux. They are confused to who you are. The council will meet in the morning."

"Why did they leave me with my animals? Is that customary of the Arapaho?"

"There is discussion that you could be a Sioux medicine woman because of how you have your

animals trained. To take your animals could bring them bad medicine. Little one, your medicine is strong, and you are unaware of your strength. I am tired and must go to bed now. Good-night," Two Rabbits got up gracefully, fading away from the fire.

Josie stood up took a deep breath of the warm night air, the intermingled scent of the smoke from the camp fires and the river. It was pleasant. The wind was blowing gently, rustling the leaves in the cotton wood, and there was the faint sound of her animals cropping grass. In the distance, there was a dog barking and murmured conversations from the village. She walked over to the Jerseys with her pail and did her nightly milking. Drank a little of the warm milk, then put a tin down by the chickens, giving them a drink and dumping the rest out on the ground. Such a waste. However, the milk that she used had saved quite a bit of supplies coming West. They wouldn't always waste the milk soon. They would be home with her Pa. Then they would have a spring house and be able to make butter and cheese.

The grass was thin under her bed roll. The ground was hard. Usually, she cuts grass, or the grass was thick enough to make for a semi-comfortable bed.

Tonight was going to be long, not just because of her bed, but because her fate would be decided tomorrow morning. She got up from her bed and stoked the fire, then began to pace the camp. Her heart was pounding; she was shaking with nervous energy. There was nothing that could be done. Josie hated the feeling of helplessness. Since her Ma had died, she had always figured something out to solve whatever problem there was to face; now, there was only a blank. Pushing the pot of coffee next to the fire to warm, she sighed loudly. Pacing the camp, lifting her arms to the star-lit sky, Josie began to speak aloud to her mother.

"Ma, I know you are in heaven right now, but I need you. I don't know if I will get out of this situation alive. Mama, help me. I am scared."

Silent tears stained Josie's cheeks. Taking a deep breath and feeling a deep hopelessness, she poured herself a cup of coffee. She took a careful sip from her cup, all too aware of how scalding hot the coffee was. Staring at her cup of coffee, she thought of her Ma. When she was little, her Ma used to make her coffee with milk…a lot of milk. It was more like milk with a splash of coffee. Over time Josie just slowly wanted less and less milk in her coffee until it was straight-up pure black coffee. Mama always drank her coffee with milk. Why Josie thought of this now, she did not know. Maybe because of missing Ma. Ma was such a strong woman. Josie sat and stared into the fire while finishing her coffee. Then returned to her bedroll for a restless night of sleep.

CHAPTER TEN:
GREAT MEDICINE

It was long before the light of morning when Josie awoke. The stars were still bright and crisp in the sky as they often are before dawn. She threw some dry leaves on the coals to stoke the fire to life. Then built the fire up with buffalo chips. Then added a little water to the coffee and set it next to the fire to slow brew. Josie led her pack train down to the river to get a drink. She had a strong compulsion to do her chores in peace, thus, the reason for waking so early. Josie did not want all the eyes of the village staring at her watering her animals. Yesterday being watched while being brought into camp was un-nerving enough. If she was going to present an image of strength, nothing could be allowed to disturb her, if that was possible. After watering the animals, Josie allowed them to graze along the water until the sun rose.

Then she ushered them back to their rope corral. While allowing the stock to graze, Josie collected a couple cups of wild seeds for her chickens. This was a task she had done numerous times on the trail. It had made her bag of scratch go farther. She milked the Jerseys. Using the milk to make breakfast, milk and cold flour creates a type of gruel. The chickens get some milk, and the rest gets dumped. Josie set about to make Grandfather's tea. Her morning was going like any other morning so far this day.

"Good morning, Grandfather. I have made some breakfast for you. Today we are eating a type of cold flour mush; it looks delicious," Josie said, holding a spoon to his lips while unconsciously holding her mouth open. Grandfather's eyes opened when he heard her voice, and he smiled. He eagerly ate every bite that Josie offered him.

After eating his last bite, Grandfather began to speak in a voice stronger than the day before, "Granddaughter, I feel a little stronger this morning. We have traveled far since leaving the spring. Where are we at?" Grandfather was becoming aware of his surroundings and did not like the state of confusion he felt or all the strangeness encircling him.

"Grandfather, we are prisoners in an Arapaho village along the Platte River. I was taking us to Fort Laramie to be with my father when we were surrounded and taken prisoner. They were going to kill us but changed their minds, but they could change their minds again. This is not a good place to be right now," Josie had wanted to lie and say everything here was fine at the Arapaho camp. She could not bring herself to lie to an aged warrior who would understand the truth.

"I heard different languages that I do not know yesterday. Granddaughter, you speak one of those languages. The other must be Arapaho since we are their prisoners."

"I speak Sioux, Grandfather. I am part of the Sioux nation from the North."

"You are Sioux, and I am Peoria. My tribe is diminished due to war and sickness. All the people that I knew are dead, the customs dying. I left the Indian lands. I am an old man. I wanted to still live while I could, not be confined to a land of death. You found me dying, saved me, and called me Grandfather. I shall always see you as my blood granddaughter, even though we are of two different nations."

"Grandfather, if we can leave this village, I plan to go to Fort Laramie to live with my father. You are welcome with us. We will have a ranch and live off the land. We can ride and explore… We will be a family," Josie was smiling at Grandfather.

"Here, Grandfather, drink your tea before it gets cold. It will help you heal. We will see what the morning brings us," he drank, not saying anything more, and slipped back into a deep sleep.

Josie needed to change Grandfather's bandages even though he had just fallen asleep. Internally, she debated whether or not she could skip changing the dressings and just let Grandfather rest. The guilt that if Josie neglected the wounds Grandfather may get ill won the internal war. She carefully lifted his shirt to access the bullet wound and removed the bandages. Josie gently bathed the wound using some hot soapy water, careful not to disturb the scabbing. To clean the scabs, she delicately dabbed the wound. The bullet wound was red and puckered around the edges. It was completely scabbed over. Josie took that as a good sign. She then put clean bandages on the wound. The slash wound on the neck was a little red and puckered; it was scabbed over and looked good. She knew if there was oozing or blood at this point

from either injury, something was wrong, and there wasn't. Grandfather was strong. Josie washed the bandages in the hot soapy water and hung them on a tree to dry to use tomorrow.

***

The council of varying chiefs and Gray-Hairs (they had no Water-Sprinkling Old Man since Many Horses died) summoned Two Rabbits, the senior-most member of the Buffalo-Lodge, to their morning meeting. Two Rabbits understood the gravity of the council she was to attend when she was summoned. The young girl's life she shared dinner with was in the balance. Everything had a soul worth recognizing. That girl's soul was unique. Two Rabbits entered the tipi where the council meeting was to take place and smiled at all in the circle. She had, in one way or another, been part of each person's life. At the council meeting was Red Feather, warrior chief. He would be expected to give an accounting of why he chose to take this girl as prisoner. What he had to say would be important to decide the girl's fate. The council would hear testimony from members of the Kit-Fox and Star-Falcons, the young braves, that were to observe the prisoner and her activities. These

activities would then be used to help determine the girl's fate.

The village chief, Spotted Turtle, looked around the circle, appraising if all crucial members of the council were present. Satisfied at the council attendance, he loudly began to hum. Other members started to hum. Once all were humming, he stopped, and so did the rest of the council. With a clear carrying voice, Spotted Turtle spoke, "Red Feather, you chose to bring the girl here a prisoner when some of your braves of the Star-Falcons wanted to kill her. There were some of your braves who spoke of letting her go on her with her travels. This is a difficult position to have dissension among your warriors. Why did you choose council as your solution?"

"The girl was puzzling to us, warriors, before we approached her because she looked like a human dressed as a white. On closer approach, the girl looked to be white. Spotted Horse went to kill the old man on the travois first when the girl spoke out in Sioux in defense of the old man. We are not at war with the Sioux. She showed bravery in this act. It was at this moment that the braves began to argue as what to do with the girl they began calling, Long Ears."

"Traditionally, animals are taken from our prisoners to prevent escape. Why were not Long Ears animals taken from her?" questioned one of the Gray-Hairs.

"Long Ears has a strong medicine over her animals. The long ear horses follow with no lead. Her cows carry cages with birds in them. Many braves thought it would be bad medicine to take her animals. I agreed with them."

"Did Long Ears try to escape with her animals, or did she respect that she was our prisoner?" the same Gray-Hair asked.

"She did not try to escape with her animals. She was instructed to make camp next to Two Rabbits lodge, and she did. I received regular reports as to activities. She cooked. She cared for the old man. She made some moccasins. She cared for her animals. She did all the thing that our women were doing in our lodges yesterday," Red Feather told the council.

"Two Rabbits, you were at her fire to eat last night," Spotted Turtled said, nodding in Two Rabbits' direction.

"Yes, the little one, Long Ears, came to my tipi inviting me to her fire to eat with her and Grandfather. She showed the greatest respect for me as an elder and guest. She showed great respect for Human elder that she cares for also."

"What did you learn about Long Ears while at her fire Two Rabbits?" Spotted Turtle asked, hoping to understand this confusing girl who was brought into camp yesterday.

"Long Ears is a Sioux girl traveling alone to her father because her mother died. The old man is an elderly human. Long Ears found him after he had been attacked and left for dead while she was traveling. Her respect for elders and life moved her to care for this human as if he was her own grandfather. The little one has powerful medicine. She is a gifted girl with an old soul that can see things clearer than most can ever dream of understanding," Two Rabbits said this last part with reverence. A compliment of that magnitude coming from someone as revered as Two Rabbits was bound to have an impact on the council. Two Rabbits meant every word she spoke about Josie. There was a gift in that girl that only comes from the divine.

Spotted Turtle looked around, sensing the impact of Two Rabbits' statement. Then he spoke, "The council would like to hear about any of Long Ears activities that we have not already heard about."

"Last night, I seen her circling her fire then, she raised her arms praying to the moon," one tribal member commented.

"I saw her drink the milk of her cow then, make an offering to the earth with the rest of the milk," chimed another tribal member.

The council circle grew silent for a moment. Spotted Turtle looked around the ring to ensure that all spoke who had anything to say. Then he spoke in his clear, strong voice, "Red Feather, you made the right choice in bringing Long Ears here for a council decision. If we, Sage-Brush People, had killed a Sioux medicine woman, this could have caused us great problems bringing us not only war with the Sioux but bad medicine. This reinforces the reason that you are warrior chief."

"Red Feather, you and two other ranked braves will escort Long Ears away from the village then, travel with her well on her way to her father. Let her know that the Arapaho, Sage-Brush People, are

friends of the Sioux. Give Long Ears the apologies of the council for delaying her travel."

"Does all council members agree with the solution on the matter of Long Ears?" No one spoke, which was the standard silent form of agreement. Speaking was done if there was a disagreement.

After a long minute of silence, "Council, may I ask something on this matter before we leave?"

"Speak Two Rabbits," Spotted Turtle said, nodding in her direction.

"I wish to accompany Long Ears when she leaves the village. I have no family left here. She has no mother. She shall need a woman, and I am lonely. I was blessed to raise fine, strong warriors. Now my tipi is empty because I had no girls. This is the daughter I always prayed for; at my age, I should say granddaughter."

"Has Long Ears asked you to accompany her?"

"No, I wish to ask her. I only wish your permission to leave if Long Ears wants my company," Two Rabbits said humbly

Spotted Turtle looked at Two Rabbits with love and said, "Two Rabbits we as a tribe we respect and honor the wishes of our elderly. Go in peace."

The night before the council meeting, Two Rabbits lying in her tipi had thought about the young girl without a mother. She had probably been six or seven years older than Josie when she lost her mother in the Cheyenne raid, but it was still hard to lose her mother even then. A mother is such an important person in a girl's life. This girl coming into adulthood still had so much to learn. There would be many changes in her life that only a woman could talk to her about. Did she know the plants here to forage, for food or medicine? She would need that knowledge. The little one needed someone to care for her. It had been too long since she had anyone to care for. The thought of caring-for a person made her feel young and alive.

The council had given her permission to leave with the girl. Two Rabbits felt a flush of happiness inside. Now, all that was needed was for the little one to agree to her becoming part of her family. It was essential to demonstrate that she was a contributor to the family and not a burden. She had a store of jerky. They could hunt or forage along the way to the little one's father. Two Rabbits

could help the little one prepares for winter. The way she lived would change, but it would be a new adventure in her late years. It would be good to be needed... to have a family.

Red Feather was striding purposefully towards Josie's camp, getting ready to speak to her, when Two Rabbits almost ran to be beside him when he spoke. Josie was just rising and smoothing her dress, preparing to speak to Red Feather, when she looked up and saw Two Rabbits' beautiful smile. Josie couldn't help but smile back at her and Red Feather also.

"You are free to leave the village. Our council extends an apology for keeping you from your journey. To ensure your safe travel, a couple of other braves and I will escort you on your way to your father. Because of the council meeting and the preparations for the journey, it is too late to leave today. Do you wish to leave in the morning?" said Two Feathers. He was hoping she would agree to leave in the morning. He could be ready with his men as fast as she could break, but he would rather have the evening with his family. The other braves and he would be gone for several days.

"Yes, morning is soon enough. I would like to leave at first light. Thank you." Josie said with a sense of relief at not being a prisoner anymore. Red Feather nodded in agreement to leave at first light. Tomorrow they would be on their way to Fort Laramie.

Red Feather turned and walked away from Josie's camp as quickly as he had arrived.

"Little one, I want to speak with you about an important matter?" Two Rabbits nervously said. She was still smiling, and her eyes were dancing with excitement.

"Sit down, Two Rabbits. Have some coffee and talk."

Two Rabbits quickly took a seat next to the fire, barely able to contain her excitement. She waited for Josie to pour their coffee before she spoke.

"I no longer wish to remain here alone with the Arapaho. It has been many seasons since my sons went to their wife's villages. The best husband a wife could ask for, Many Horses, has also been gone for many seasons. I wish to go with you and Grandfather then I will no longer be alone. When I was young, I would pray for a daughter. Now it

seems *Okaga* has given me the chance to be a grandmother to you. I will help you and teach you things. I will help you prepare for winter. I can help cook and care for the lodge. I can do many things to lighten your burden, little one," Two Rabbits tried to stay calm and meter out her words carefully instead of pouring them out like an over flooded river after a storm.

"What about your tipi? We could not take it. Do you have a horse to ride?" As she asked about the horse, Josie immediately realized that this was a foolish question. The plains people were born in the saddle, it seemed. This idea of Two Rabbits coming with her and Grandfather was not something that Josie had prepared herself for when thinking of possible events for this day.

"I will give my tipi to a newlywed couple in the village. I have many horses. I take two good horses with me. The others I will gift, *Wakan Tanka,* blessing our travels for the generosity. One horse can carry my travois with my things. The other I will ride. Does this mean I can go with you, little one?" Two Rabbits had a wistful look on her face.

"Yes, if this is what you want, you may come with us. We will live differently than you are used to

right now. We will live in a house and not a tipi. We won't always be moving with the seasons. I just don't want you to get bored and miss your old life here."

"Thank you…thank you, little one. I am ready for the changes this journey will bring. Now I must go. There is a lot I must do before first light tomorrow," Two Rabbits left with a dainty little prance towards her tipi. She felt like a young woman again, just starting anew; too bad her body didn't recognize how young her soul was.

Josie wasn't sure if she had made the right decision about Two Rabbits. How could she leave Two Rabbits here alone? Last winter had been awful for Josie without her family. Two Rabbits has been without her family for years. That had to be torturous. The tribe respected Two Rabbits and took care of her needs, but it was not the same as having a family. Josie thought of all the long hours Two Rabbits sat alone in her tipi; it was sad. Pa wouldn't mind. He had a soft spot for elderly people, at least that is what Ma had said. Ma had told a story about her grandfather, Josie's great grandfather, of how her Pa would always bring him tobacco and dried apples because that made him happy. Josie realized that it would take more

food to feed her growing family. Well, what use was it being a good hunter if you didn't have people to feed? Josie was a good hunter. Pa would help too. Everything would work out fine.

First light came, Josie had her pack train ready to depart the village. Two Rabbits fell in behind her with two horses with a well-loaded travois. Then they were joined by Red Feather and two other braves. Red Feather led the way. Josie followed the other two braves flanked the rear of the procession. The air hinted of impending rain, the patches of grass smelt fresh under the feet of the horses and sage brush faint scent was always present. The pack train dragging the two travoises was throwing up a cloud of dust. This was the way the whole day went after leaving the Arapaho camp, completely uneventful.

The braves stayed through the second day of travel. Then on the morning of the third day of travel, they turned back, returning to their village. Their departure must have been a sign to mother nature to let it rain. It rained on and off for the next two days on the trail creating a slow-moving clay-footed mess. The travois would dig into the clay in places like a plow; in others places, the travois would glide like they were on ice. The rain did not

slow the pack train's travel any. They saw a wagon train on the other side of the river slogging along their wheels, digging into the mud. The travois of the pack train pulled more like a sled, so they just kept going forward.

Grandfather, during these days, grew more robust and, in the evening, would sit by the fire visiting with Two Rabbits and Josie. The conversations usually focused on what the future would hold for all of them. There were times they spoke of the plants and animals they had seen during the day. They would harvest some plants to eat, such as lambs quarter and wild onions. The days after the rain, the terrain quickly grew drier and dustier. The dust clung to their bodies and all over the pack train. There was more sage brush and prickly pear the further west they traveled. Two Rabbits showed them how to eat prickly pear by burning off the spines then slicing and eating raw. It tasted similar to a cucumber. She said they could be cooked. They could be also be used as medicine to treat wounds.

They had passed Fort Bernard a few hours back. They joyfully pressed forward, knowing they were close to their destination. Coming over a small sage-covered ridge, they spotted Fort Laramie on

the tenth day out of the Arapaho camp. It was getting late. The sky was beginning to show the rainbow of evening splendor. They were a good mile away still. The air hung heavy with impending rain. Exhausted, the travelers decided to set camp under some cotton wood trees. It had been a long hard few days pushing for Fort Laramie. Now they were here, much to their relief. Josie pushed her pack train harder than she usually would have, knowing that they were close to their new home. Two Rabbits made a light dinner while Josie tended the animals. It would be easier for Josie to go into the fort early in the morning and inquire about her father. They would still probably need to travel a bit to get to Pa's ranch. This would give them plenty of daylight. Josie finally relaxed a little and studied the backdrop of Fort Laramie...there were mountains far away.

No sooner had she rolled into her bed roll exhaust from the hard travel when a gentle rain began to fall. The sage smelt sweet from the rain, and the air was a little crisp. Josie lay in her bedroll thinking how wonderful it would be to see Pa again. It has almost been two years since seeing her Pa. Ma and she didn't expect him to be gone so long, but maybe some things take longer than expected. Her trip had sure taken longer than expected. First, the chick pox laid her up, then finding Grandfather, then the Arapahoe village. These three things had cost her a couple weeks. Josie had hoped to beat the first of the wagon trains to Fort Laramie, but because of the delays, she was arriving at the same time as some of the earlier wagon trains. This didn't matter because they were finally here. Tomorrow she would see her Pa.

CHAPTER ELEVEN: FORT LARAMIE

The sky was a light hazed over gray when they broke camp. It was still gently raining on and off. The air was cool, almost cold. The short distance to Fort Laramie was quickly traversed by the well-seasoned pack train. Josie had no plan to find her Pa once at Fort Laramie. Her focus had been simply to arrive at Fort Laramie. Now standing in front of all the buildings with her pack train, she lacked action. This was a military fort; maybe the best place to start would be to speak to whoever was in command. Then he can point her in the right direction for information. Leading her pack train to the side of a building out of the way. Josie got off her horse and ground hitched it. That good horse of hers wasn't going anywhere without her, but she tied it out of precaution. Two Rabbits followed, without questions, trusting Josie's

decisions here at the fort because she was entirely out of her element.

"Two Rabbits, I am going to find the head soldier, the commander. Hopefully, he will be able to give me information on my father. Will you look after Grandfather while I am gone?" Josie said.

"Little one, we will be fine here. You find out what you need to from the soldier. I will make Grandfather and me some coffee and wait. There is no hurry. We are old and patient," She smiled encouragingly at Josie with sparkly eyes.

"Hopefully, I find out where father is quickly. Then we can be on our way to him. I can't wait for him to meet you and Grandfather. Our family will finally be all together," Josie going to leave, turned and gave Two Rabbits a quick hug.

***

The little one is such a kind-hearted girl. Her father has to be as well. It would be awful if he did not accept Grandfather and herself. Over the trail, she had begun to bond with her new family, and it would be difficult to lose them. Filling the coffee pot from the canteen and adding coffee…good thing there were dry buffalo chips on her travois,

now the coffee could be made. Too many times had she wished for dry fire start in her life, that now she carried some. It was nice that all of them spoke English. It allowed them to talk freely and not struggle to communicate. Now and then, there is a word to learn that is expected. There are many soldiers, and they watch us as if we are going to do something. Can they not see we are old? Maybe they wonder why we are with the white girl? If the soldiers want to know, they can ask. We will sit and drink our coffee and wait.

***

Two Rabbits is a good woman. She does well to take care of Granddaughter and himself. What an excellent woman to produce buffalo chips to make coffee. Her planning is good. The stronger that he is, the more time he has had to get to know Granddaughter and Two Rabbits. It was a good choice for Two Rabbits to join the family Granddaughter is going to need a woman. There are things that her father and he would not know how to explain or teach or handle to a young woman. No, a girl needs a woman…a good woman. Granddaughter is strong and brave but has much to learn. She is still a child. When strength returns to this body, he will help Granddaughter

with her work and hunting. We will do these things together.

***

Anxiously Josie walked in front of the buildings looking for a sign of where to go to speak to someone in charge. She walked up and down the building fronts probably a half dozen times before a squat square face soldier came up to her.

"Can I help you find something, miss?"

"Yes, please, I want to speak to whoever is in charge of the fort."

"I guess that would be the commander. That would be Colonel Amos, miss."

"Where can I find this Colonel Amos?"

"He rode in yesterday from a campaign. He should be in his office. I could escort you there if you like."

"Please. I have traipsed several times up and down this fort trying to figure out where to go."

"Where are you from, miss? I am from Iowa came out here as a group of volunteer soldiers. That

way, some of the regular soldiers could go fight the war."

"I am from Illinois. The war started?

"Yep. After the Confederates fired on Fort Sumter. Us new troops have only been here a week. By the way, my name is George Harris" he stuck out his hand to shake Josie's hand.

"My name is Josie Tormey. It's a pleasure to meet you, Mr. Harris," she said, shaking George's hand.

"Mr. Harris, how did you folk know about the war so soon?"

"We have a telegraph back home that we get the news over. There is a telegraph down in Denver also, and there will be a telegraph here within a few months."

"Civilization progressed this far out on the frontier. It is amazing."

"Miss, this is the Colonel's office. Be seeing you around."

Josie stepped up to the freshly painted gray door and knocked.

"Come in and be quick about it," snapped a voice from within.

Stepping in hesitantly into the clean office. Josie noticed the overly stuffed shelves bulging with books. The orderly desk and the man behind the desk were in complete contrast to the room. He was an older middle-aged man, probably fifty, with balding brown disheveled hair, unshaven, and his shirt was stained with coffee, but he had bright blue eyes that had deep laugh lines at the corners. His intensely blue eyes gave Josie the confidence to find her voice.

"Sir, I came here looking for help finding my Pa. I have a letter that says that he found a place around Fort Laramie to start a ranch. He should be a local."

"Well, miss, what is yours and your father's name? That will help me help you," his kindly eyes were sparkling, and his voice took on a gentle, lyrical tone.

"My name is Josephine Tormey, Josie for short. My Pa's is Jefferson Tormey."

"Josie, where is your mother? I want to speak with her?" The colonel looked a little concerned.

"Sir, my Ma died. I came out here on my own to be with Pa. I found Grandfather and Grandmother along the way," Josie took the liberty of calling Two Rabbits, Grandmother, to signify her importance.

"Incredible. I want to speak to you about something important; however, I want to hear your story first. Did you have problems? It must have been difficult being a girl on her own coming over the trail."

The colonel walked over to the stove in the room while grabbing two blue tin cups off a shelf. Then proceeded to pour two cups of coffee, handing one to Josie. Then, he sat down in his chair at his desk. Josie was seated comfortably across the desk from the colonel. Josie began her story with her mother's death and finished it with her arrival there at Fort Laramie. It had been in her mind to skip the part about the ferryman; however, she felt compelled to tell the colonel every detail of her journey, good or bad.

"That is a remarkable story, young lady. You made several difficult decisions in planning to come West. You did what had to be done to survive in dealing with the ferryman. Being ill and caring for

yourself showed strength. You show fortitude and wisdom beyond your years in handling the Arapaho. Then take on yourself to care for a wound Indian with limited knowledge. Do you think these Ed and Col men are somewhere on the trail still looking for you?"

"I don't know where Ed and Col are at. I hope to never see them again. They are nothing but trouble. You said you needed to speak to me about something important, Colonel."

"Josie, I needed to hear your story to know how to handle this situation. Your father bought four sections of land and filed it with Omaha. Do you know how big a section is?" Josie nodded her head no. "I didn't think so. A section is a square mile. So, your Pa bought four square miles. That cost a pretty penny. He also bought a hundred head of cattle for his place. I know he was just getting started. Did you know your father had a brother named Andrew or Andy?"

"I have met my Uncle Andy a few times. Pa said he was a riverboat gambler, so we didn't see him much. Ma didn't like him. She thought he was a bad influence on me. How do you know about my Uncle Andy?"

"Gamblers tend to follow the money. Andy was probably out here because of the gold camps. Back to what I was originally trying to tell you. Andy ran into your father when he went to Denver to buy some cattle. Andy showed up out here a few months later. He was angry because your Pa wouldn't give him any money to go back to Denver. Andy must have figured your father for being mighty rich. He began yelling at your father about hoarding his inheritance and not sharing with his older brother. He was causing quite the scene. Your Pa got tired of listening to him and turned around to walk away. Well…Andy shot him in the back. This was witnessed by dozens, right here at the fort."

"My Pa is dead? What about Uncle Andy?" Josie blurted in a panicked wave of shock.

"We buried your Pa outside the fort last November. I have his personal effects in a file, along with a record of death since it happened here at the fort. I didn't know where to write, but I knew he had a family. As for Andy, he lit a shuck within seconds of the shooting. We chased him, then a blizzard hit, and we lost all tracks."

"I hope I don't see Uncle Andy because I might have to kill him," a deep black anger was over Josie. They sat in silence for several minutes, drinking their coffee. Time was needed to process the news of the murder. The anger and the pain were written all over Josie's face. Tears started to well, then retreated.

"Do you want me to make arrangements for you to return to the states?" the colonel asked gently, looking Josie in the eyes.

"I have nothing and no one there," she sat silent for a moment pushing back tears.

"The only choice I see is to move forward. The ranch is mine now. All this way across the trail, I have been dreaming about is a ranch with my Pa. Well, there still is the ranch. Do you know where it is, Colonel?" with a deep audible breath and a look of determination, Josie asked.

"I do know where it is at. I helped your father file his papers for the land patent. It is about a hundred miles away from the fort. That is a long way from here. There is a stage station about forty miles away on Brown Creek from your place, but it is just a place to change horses."

"Grandfather, Grandmother, and I will be fine on the ranch alone. We are going to need some supplies before we head to the ranch. I don't know what my Pa has over there. I want enough supplies for winter in case we don't get back to the fort until spring," she said this more thinking aloud than for the Colonel's benefit.

"Josie, I would like to help you if you are determined to go to the ranch to live. Let me assign two scouts to take you to the ranch. I will assign two other soldiers to help you with collecting your supplies. We carry most everything Fort Bernard does, but if you like, you could go to Fort Bernard."

"Thank you for the help. I will do my shopping here. It will make life easier having guides to the ranch and people to help with the shopping. I don't have a wagon or any oxen to haul the supplies. Could this be procured for me?"

"Easily settlers are always leaving tired oxen. By next spring, they are in fine shape. A wagon is a simple request. Is there anything else that you need help with, Josie?" smiling at the girl's strength.

"Books. Where can I get books? If I am at the ranch over the winter. I definitely want a few books."

"I will personally collect you a couple of boxes of books from around the fort. Another thing other than oxen the wagon trains tend to dispose of here is books, along with heavy furniture they decide not to haul over the mountains. One wagon may not be enough because you are setting up house. If it is not, one of the scouts can drive one of the fort's extra wagon and bring it back to the fort."

"That is generous of you, Colonel. There are several extra things I would like to purchase this trip that I normally wouldn't buy."

"How are you set in funds?" furrows above his brows.

"I am fine for now. I need to look towards the future and bring in an income. No matter how small it is, it will help. Does the Army purchase goods from civilians like cheese, eggs, butter, and meat?" Josie had been thinking about trading with the fort as possible income all the way across the trail.

"We do purchase fresh goods like you mentioned."

"Then, when I come to the fort, I will bring a stock of what I have on hand. I know I will have cheese and maybe eggs. Would you consider taking smoked meat it is easier to transport?"

"We don't get much-smoked meat. It is usually salted or jerked. It would be a nice change around here."

"Colonel, I think we have a business deal," Josie stood to leave.

"Wait outside, and I'll have a couple of soldiers to help you, Josie."

***

What a strong girl. Here he anticipated a flood of tears and womanly hysterics, yet she pushed back the tears and thought of killing the man who killed her father. That girl had grit. Then she is going out into the wilderness to live on a ranch she has never seen. That girl has probably never ranched a day in her life, but she is game. Has horse sense enough in her grief to plan for supplies for the winter...just in case she doesn't get back to the fort. If that wasn't enough, she made a business deal to ensure she would have some income. I knew Jefferson was a remarkable man. His wife must have been

something amazing. Their child is the strength that is going to build this frontier.

***

Josie waited outside the colonel's office, thinking about everything that needed to be purchased. She needed focus, and the only way to do that was to push the anger and sorrow deep down inside, breathe because she felt like she was smothering, and work. Working had always helped her think and calm down. They were going to the ranch for a year; she needed to focus. This was supply shopping on a large scale. Having an idea of how much Mama put away each winter for each of them helped guide the list. There were other things like candles and sheeting. They needed extra pots and pails for making cheese. Would they have cheese presses? Probably not she would have to make some. Blankets, it would be cold. Extra barrels and jars to store goods in because sacked goods would get bugs and rodents. A butter churn was needed and a couple of crocks for storage. Medical supplies: long forceps (in case she ever needs to pull anything out again), Laudanum, whiskey, mint, camphor. The only way to do this right was to write a list under categories to ensure

everything got bought because there was no going back to town for an item.

The square face soldier named George and another soldier with a thin-lipped grin walked up to Josie.

"Hello, Mr. Harris, are you here to help me with my shopping?"

"You don't have to call me Mr. Harris. George works just fine, and this is John. The colonel said that we were to take care of everything you needed and to make sure that no one gave you or your grandparents a difficult time while here at the fort."

"Do you think the grandparents will be unmolested while we take care of business? I was just getting ready to walk over to them and explain we are getting supplies together. Would you like to meet them?"

"Sure, I love my grandparents. They live on a farm next to ours back home. We were always back and forth, helping one another with things. Grandpa was always spinning a yarn about one thing or another. My grandma's bread was always so light and tasty with butter and strawberry jam," George said.

They rounded the side of the building. There was Two Rabbits sitting on a blanket on the ground drinking her coffee, and Grandfather propped up on the travois also drinking coffee. George immediately smiled at the elderly Indians. John's face looked as if he had been hit with a sack full of manure. John's expression was not lost on Josie. She was sure that Two Rabbits and Grandfather had seen the look also. Some whites just hate Indians.

"Grandfather and Grandmother," Josie said, looking at Two Rabbits, who smiled broadly at hearing herself being referred to as "grandmother." "This is George and John; they have been assigned by the Colonel to help me get the supplies we need to go to the ranch. The ranch is about a hundred miles away from here. We will rest here unbothered. When we leave, two Army scouts are going with us to show us to the ranch."

"We have one extra cup if one of you wants coffee?" Grandmother offered the soldiers.

"No, thank you, ma'am. We need to get started rounding up these supplies for Miss Josie and you all. I appreciate the offer," George said with a smile.

"The first thing I need is a wagon and oxen. Otherwise, we won't be able to load the supplies."

"We can get that for you. You can pay the livery man for the wagon and oxen when you're at the store. The livery is next door," George quickly replied.

"Then would you gentlemen mind if I sit here and write a shopping list and drink a cup of coffee?" Her eyes pleading.

"No problem Miss Josie. This will take us about an hour. The oxen are far off in the pasture," George spoke, still smiling.

Josie takes a piece of paper and pencil from her pack. It was vital for her to focus on a list of what they would need at the ranch. Accepting a cup of coffee from Grandmother, she began to quickly write. It was important to not forget a few things that would just make their lives pleasant. Her list was made, and the soldiers were not back. She was sure it had been at least a couple of hours because she had lingered on her list, not wanting to forget essential items. Since the soldiers had not returned, Josie went about setting camp right where they were, right next to the building. If people didn't like it, they could go fork a bronc. She was not

moving the Grandparents. After the news she just got about her Pa, it was all she could do to keep her composure.

"Hey, you can't set camp there?" A soldier came over and said to Josie.

"Go speak to Colonel Amos if you have a problem. We are here until the scouts escort us to our ranch." Josie told the soldier with hands on her hips and much more attitude than was necessary.

The soldier never came back. No other soldier said anything about them camping where they were. George returned to Josie's camp with a different gangly soldier with a big nose and a bigger smile.

"Parked the wagon over at the store. That way, we can load as you purchase. By the way, this is Paul," George declared when making eye contact with Josie.

"What happened to John?" Josie asks curiously.

"Seemed John had some problem helping you and your family. The colonel, on hearing his complaint, assigned him to a new special assignment... the business end of the shovel in the livery stable for a week." George laughed.

"I made my list, gentleman, and we just may need a second wagon. I am setting up house, and I don't think there is much at the ranch other than probably a house."

"If we need a second wagon, that will be easy since we will be using one of the commands. We'll just hook a couple horses to it until we go fetch a few more oxen. We will get everything taken care of just fine, Miss Josie. Won't we, Paul?"

"No problem. We will get you packed good in tight and lashed down properly so you won't have any problems getting out to your ranch," Paul said, nodding his head in agreement.

"Do you think that the two of you can handle the loading by yourselves?"

"Sure. That's what the Army trains us for…to be strong," George chuckles again.

Josie strode across the compound to the store with George and Paul with list in hand. It wasn't like the stores that she had seen back East. As soon as the door to the store was opened, the smell of leather, tobacco, spices, and a certain earthiness assaulted your nose. This place was a jumbled mess of every item imaginable. The store seemed to wander off into tunnels of goods. Everywhere something different to see. Since this was a store out on the frontier, she was expecting the store to carry on a scant few items. Before going to the counter to speak to anyone, Josie wanders the store studying various things. One of the items that caught her attention was a new "Henry .44 Repeating Rifle." That was all the sign said about the rifle, but it was beautiful. It would be a good idea to have an extra gun around the ranch. She would have to speak to someone about it…maybe.

"Howdy, young lady, what can I help you with today?"

"I need a lot of supplies because I am heading to my ranch with my grandparents, and I want supplies for a year. I don't know when I will get back to the fort. I would rather have more than not enough. I also need household goods because I sold out back East and came out here with just a couple pack critters. I need just about everything."

"It's the beginning of the wagon train season, so I still have plenty of supplies. The wagons haven't had a chance to wipe me out. One of the good things about them trains they always bring interesting things to trade. You never know what them greenhorn emigrants will bring, sure make for an interesting store. I always make the trades because someone will come along and buy what I traded for."

"Yes, I see that you have quite a store here. I almost don't know where to start with my list with so many things to look at in here."

"I see you have a list. Why don't we start there, dear, alright?"

"That is a good idea. What is a barrel of flour going for out here?"

"A barrel of flour is $7.61, a little higher than the states."

"That price is not as bad as I was expecting. Here is the list."

***

5 Barrels Flour	100lb. Corn Meal	100qt. Beans
50lb. Sugar	50lb. Rice	50lb. Coffee
50lb. Soap	30lb. Salt	1lb. Baking Powder
Cinnamon	Vanilla	Black Pepper
30lb. Dried Apples	20lb. Dried Vegetable	200lb. Bacon
1 Barrel Vinegar	5lb. Rock Candy	Dried Peppers

Josie's Journey: Trail of Change

Forceps	Laudanum	Whiskey
Mint	Camphor	Mineral Oil

6 Blankets	6 Metal Pails	2 Cheese Press
Pots	Metal Dishes	Butter Churn
Utensils	Thread	Needles
20yrs. Sheeting	Knives	2 Butter Crocks
20 Bx. Matches	12 Jars	6 Barrels
400 Candles	2 Candle Holders	Pitch Fork
Hoe	Saw	Hand Plane
2 Shovels	Rake	20lb. Nails
Hammer	Hatchet	Mallet
10lb. Powder	500 Ball	300lb. Chicken Scratch
Scythe	Snath	2 Augers
6 Canvas'	Auger Brace	2 Chisels
2 Wash Tubs	Wash Board	Hand Mangler
Clothes Pins	Clothes Line	Flour Sifter

***

"This is quite a list, little miss…I believe I have everything on your list. I knew I would eventually sell those cheese presses. I have two more cheese presses; do you want them?"

"I think that I can use them. When I came into the store and was browsing, something else that caught my attention was the Henry rifle. Can you tell me about it?

"A lot of people look at that rifle. Its nickname is the "Sixteen-Shooter." This here rifle takes these new .44 cartridges. No ball and powder. Sixteen shots without needing to load. Remarkable, isn't it?" The robust bald man was smiling, turning the gun over in his hands.

"How accurate is it? I use a Kentucky Long Rifle. And what does it cost?"

"It is accurate as your Kentucky, I suppose. I want $20 and $2 for 200 rounds."

"Um…does it have a case?" Josie asked in deep contemplation.

"Yep, sure does."

"Add it to my order. Is there anything that I missed?"

"Not unless you're looking for luxury. I have a few pillows and quilts. I even have a brand new cookstove if you're interested. Some greenhorn hauled a huge stove over the trail. Played out his

team getting here. He realized there was no way he was going over the mountains without lightning the load. You should have seen the crying his wife was doing."

"I'd take a look at the stove. A stove isn't just for cooking. It heats a house better than a fireplace. First, is it a woodstove or one of them city stoves that only use coal? A coal stove where I am going wouldn't do me any good."

"Let's take a look at it. It should say what type of fuel to use in the stove," he said, walking to the back of the store to a big stove that had multiple burners and an oven.

Josie could see walking up to the stove that it was a wood stove. It had an attached kindling rack on the side. This was nicer than her Mama's stove. This stove had an enamel coating meaning it didn't have to be blacked except the top. This was a brand-new top-of-the-line stove. No wonder that woman had cried. She had tried not to act too excited. Josie opened the oven door and moved a few grates.

"It is a wood-burning stove… it could work. It is a little big, though…." Josie started to walk away.

"I will sell you the stove for $18. That's the cost of a smaller stove."

"I don't know. I would still need the chimney pipe...."

"I throw that in for a dollar."

"I'll take the stove. Can you load it with everything else?" Josie was beyond overjoyed. She knew that stove was worth every bit of $30 because of the ads in the newspapers she had seen back East.

George and Paul were waiting out front of the store for Josie. The sky was still overcast, but the rain had temporally stopped, and the two soldiers looked content. They were in for their share of work with that order that was just made. She realized that a significant dent was just made in her cache of money. Not every day are you going to have to set up house, though. It was nerve-racking to spend that large amount of money. Her parents didn't deal with cash very often in front of her. They mostly worked in trade. This was a step out of her comfort area. Nothing to do about it now but move forward.

"I am sorry, gentlemen, that I have bought the store out. We are going to need a second wagon," Josie said with a genial smile.

"Miss, we were just standing here talking about what had to be on that list of yours, and well…" Paul gestures at the second wagon.

"Another soldier went to retrieve another couple yoke of oxen," George said with his ever-present smile.

The soldiers went to task loading the wagons. Josie continued to browse the store and added a few items to order. The quilts were beautiful, the colors and patterns were happy and homey. They were $.75 apiece; she added four to the order. The pillows were only $.12; she added six to the order. There were a few kitchen items like a strainer, whisk, mixing bowls, cheesecloth, rolling pin, dishpans. A few things to make life easier. They did have dried rennet. She didn't expect they would. Lastly, adding more fabric to her order. While looking, it dawned on her that they needed ticking for mattresses cloth to make clothes. The sheeting had been planned to make towels, bandages, and miscellaneous items. Now she doubled it to make sheets for the beds. This was so complicated to think about off the top of her head. When making the list, she tried to reflect on what she sold before coming over the trail and what she used every day at home. This was the best that could be done for now. There was no need for her to wait here while the wagons were loaded. Take a moment to pay both the store and the livery. She needed to check with the colonel to make sure they could leave at first light and get those books.

"Colonel Amos… it is me, Josie. Can I come in, sir?" Josie asked.

"Come in, Josie. How are all the preparations going, young lady? Colonel Amos' eyes twinkling and a toothy smile emerged from the thick bush of his whiskers.

"Thank you for all the help you and your soldiers are giving us. It will be quite the task to unload once at the ranch. I came to get the boxes of books to get loaded with the mound of other things. I would like to leave at first light for the ranch. Will your scouts be able to leave then?"

"The scouts will be ready at first light. I also took the liberty of sending the books already over to your wagon. I had started thinking about you unloading already? I thought of my daughter

unloading a wagon…well, that is just not acceptable. Are the two men I sent to help you load courteous and respectful?" In the back of his mind, he was thinking about Private John Jenkins and his issue with helping Josie's Indian grandparents from earlier today.

"Yes, they are both nice. The soldiers are good workers also."

"Good, that is what I wanted to hear. Those two men will accompany you and the scouts to the ranch. They can drive your wagons and unload them for you when you arrive."

"Sir, that is beyond generous of you. Thank you. But don't they have duties here that need attending?"

"They are both new here. It will do them good to get the lay of the land. The route to your ranch is a shortcut to the Salt Lake stage. Occasionally, I send riders that way. Some experienced travelers out here take that way to Salt Lake rather than going over to South Pass. They say it's faster. It will do those men good to help you and learn the route," the colonel said this, leaning back in his chair.

"I studied my map here of the area with my scouts, and I told you a hundred miles to your ranch, it is less. I noted where your father's home is when your father and I last visited and marked it on the map for reference. I do this with all the locals. You are about eighty miles from the ranch; that's a day less travel."

"A day adds up if I come back and forth to the fort. Do you know anything else about the ranch?"

"I only know that your father said he was just getting started. I don't know what he meant by that, dear."

"I just don't know anything about ranching. I'll learn, though, and I don't know what Pa has got done on the ranch either."

"Your father said he had been busy. It will be fine. If you need help, ask."

"Thank you, colonel. I will see you next time I am at the fort."

***

How could such a young girl be so strong? He just wanted to take care of her. Keep her here at the fort where she would be safe. Even as he thought this, he knew it was impossible. She was an independent creature. That is part of what he liked about her. The colonel was sending this help now as his only means of supporting this young lady in her forward vision. The assistance was offered in the future but doubted that Josie would ever ask. There was a lot of hard work ahead of her, plus caring for the grandparents. He would have the scouts give him a report about the ranch?

 This dear girl reminded him so much of his daughter, Evelyn, who died from Cholera. The Cholera epidemic struck St. Louis in 1849, where his daughter was going to school at *Visitation Academy.* She was living with a retired officer and his wife, his friends. It was difficult to leave her there in St. Louis; however, he had just been commissioned to the New Mexico Territory to Fort Defiance in the middle of Indian lands. Evelyn wanted to go so badly, always full of adventure and wanderlust. This was just not a post that he could think about taking his cherished daughter. If she had taken her, maybe she would still be here. She should have been safe at school. Thinking about her won't bring her back. Evelyn would want him to watch out for the parentless girl with the adventurous spirit.

***

The first wagon had already been loaded and parked by Josie's camp when she walked up to sit next to Grandmother. Grandfather was sleeping. He had been awake most of the day, which was good. This meant he was stronger. Pouring herself a cup of coffee and reclining on her saddle Josie for the first time today, had a chance to think about the events of the day. There had been no time to fully process her father's murder. She was so angry! Her stomach was churning, heart pounding. She wanted to throw herself down and have one dandy of a conniption fit because of the sorrow she felt… but wouldn't. Things had to be done. It had been that way when her mother died, also. Life doesn't stop because someone dies. It only complicates life for the living. The grandparents still needed her to be strong and carry-on…and what else would she do? Giving up wasn't an option. *No matter what, the cows need milked, and the chores need done.*

CHAPTER TWELVE: FAMILY TIES

"Col, I have just seen that dang gum girl with the horses we been hunting clear across the country," Ed said, running back into the livery excited.

"You saw that little whelp with the pack train from Independence?" Col asks, shocked as he continues currying his horse. Honestly, he almost forgot about her and was content currying his horse. He also knew how bad Ed wanted this girl.

"Yep, the same one. Except now she has a couple ancient Indians with her with a couple cayuses," Ed smiling like he found the mother lode.

"Maybe we should just mosey over to her camp and see if she could use our assistance in managing her affairs," Col said with a menacing smile.

***

John, the whole time doing his begrudged shovel duty in the livery stable, eavesdropped on the entire conversation between Ed and Col. He figured they had to be talking about that Josie girl and those filthy Indians she called "Grandparents." There was no one else here at the fort that fit that description. "Can't believe the colonel actually ordered me to help them," John grumbled under his breath. It was all their fault that he was stuck mucking out stalls. His shirt was soaked with sweat, and nostrils filled with the stagnate aroma of fresh manure, straw, and horseflesh. Why would the colonel care about some Indian loving girl when we're at war with the Indians? The colonel must be plain loco. He hoped those side-winders took care of the Indian infestment at the fort. Hope those two men had a good plan. That Josie flaunting her money around here at the fort. Everyone was talking about her two wagons. How does a young girl and a couple dirty Indians come by all that money? All my family had was a little dirt-sod hut that hardly produced enough to survive on; look at her with her wealth. Wish he could help this Ed and Col with this Indian problem. He's here to fight Indians… not clean stalls.

***

Dinner had been finished and cleaned up. Josie's family was sitting around the fire drinking the last of their coffee. The grandparents knew they were leaving in the morning for the ranch. The grandparents did not know that Josie's father was dead, let alone murdered by her uncle. She could tell them when they got to the ranch. She needed to process her grief in private. Grandfather would be up riding a horse before long. The only reason he still rode the travois was the gun wound when walking or sitting straight-up for any time became painful. He still had not told the story of the attack before when he was found at the willows. The mood was calm around the fire; the family was excited to be on the last leg of their journey. The grandparents couldn't believe all the supplies that they would be leaving with the morning. They were full of questions about what had been bought. Both their eyes sparkling with wonder and joy. They were all going to be fine. Josie was getting ready to turn in when she smelt something pungent suddenly and heard a noise for some reason; it made her nervous. She stood up casually as if to get more coffee and kept listening.

Lingering behind one of Josie's wagons, Col and Ed were lurking, assessing the situation around the fire. They both smelled of Indian Whiskey and tobacco. They didn't see any rifles anywhere. Good, they were defenseless! Ed thought that the old Indian man looked familiar. There were not any soldiers standing guard where the camp could be observed. What was a little girl and two ancient Indians going to do against them? One of their boots scraped on the gravel, making a noise. Neither thought anyone in the camp had heard anything. They had been working together for so long they had confidence in each other. They each do their job, they both profit. This was an old game to them, to stalk out their prey.

"Well, imagine running into you out here without your tough friend?" Ed stated, stepping into the firelight.

"Please sit down and have some coffee," Josie said without missing a beat. She recognized Ed immediately. She needed to stall him so she could think for a second. His presence could only equal death, not only for her but the Grandparents. She was not going to allow Ed to kill them.

"We're not here on any social call," Col said, coming from the shadows.

"Why else would you gentleman come calling then?" trying to look completely naïve. Now she knew both of them were here. That was going to make things more difficult for her.

"We come here to…to right a wrong done to us in Independence by you," Col stammered. He was utterly bewildered. Why was she acting like they were going to have tea? Maybe it was because she was just a kid. They could just rob her, and they wouldn't need to kill her because she wouldn't fight back. He hated the killing part. That's why Ed always handled that part of the plan.

"I am so sorry to have wronged you, gentlemen," Josie lavished and batted her eyes. She was trying hard to look clueless to their intent.

"I'm tired of this let's just kill them and leave," Ed blurted.

Josie didn't need to hear anymore. She had only been stalling for time to position herself better to reach her rifle, under the edge of her bedroll. During the brief conversation, she had casually slipped her hand into her dress pocket, grasping the hilt of her Bowie knife. At the mention of "killing them," her hand swiftly came out of her pocket, and the knife was sailing across the fire straight at Col. The knife was thrown with such force it went into Col's gut all the way to the hilt. As she let the knife fly, Josie dove for her rifle. She did this in one fluid action. Out of the corner of her eye, she saw Ed raise a gun and fire. Josie felt her arm swing back, pulling her body with the momentum. She didn't even flinch when she felt the impact and burning sensation of the hot lead. Josie was focused on Ed; her rifle was lifted and fired haphazardly at Ed in a fluid motion. She did not know if she had hit him or not. There had been no time to aim properly.

Josie dropped her gun; she didn't have time to reload. Jumping up to retrieve her Bowie knife. Grandmother already had the Bowie and had stabbed Col again, in the heart this time. Josie heard multiple hurried footsteps coming towards them. Ed had disappeared. Turning back to her rifle to load it, Grandfather was already doing that task. Soldiers appeared around the fire, wanting to know what happened. The colonel crowded his way to the fire and looked at Josie, who was bleeding. The Grandmother was cleaning a knife in the dirt sitting peacefully, and Grandfather was sitting holding a rifle with a slight grin.

"What in tarnation just happened here?" the colonel yelled, quieting all the soldiers.

"I told you about Ed and Col. Well, there is Col," Josie said, pointing at the body of Col next to the fire.

"Where is Ed?"

"He disappeared. I don't know if I hit him or not when I fired. I didn't have time to aim proper. I just had to shoot," Josie's face was flush, and she felt nauseous all of a sudden but was trying to look composed. Her arm was really starting to hurt worse by the moment.

"Josie, you have been hit. We better get you mended up, and you can tell me the whole story," the colonel looked almost faint for a moment. This was not Evelyn; still, it was a precious girl with a bullet wound in his fort right under his guard's watch was enough to infuriate him.

"I want you two men to stand guard here tonight. In the morning, we are going hunting for a man who would attack a young lady and her

Grandparents," the colonel pointed and bellowing out his orders.

***

The colonel could not believe that this Col and Ed would have the gumption to attack Josie and her grandparents while her at his fort. It was an insult that any road agent would try an attack within his fort's boundaries. He should have that pot-licker drawn and quartered when he caught that Ed. That girl has impressed him again, handling those two renegades like a seasoned fighter. What sand! She heard steps on the gravel that alerted her to something, only seconds before the attack. That is one level head on her shoulders. After hearing how the attack occurred, it is impressive how the grandparents jumped up to do their part. They make a fine family… a fine engineered unit. It was amazing how Josie could throw a knife. She has been practicing for almost a year because she thought it was a neat trick. Wonder what other talents we will see that she just takes for granted as just being herself. Josie is a dynamic person. Oh, if his Evelyn was alive, she would dote on Josie. Both cut from the same strong free spirit.

***

Ed came running into the livery, blood saturating his shirt. He felt his vision fading in and out. Ed had to get out of there; these soldier boys would be looking for him before long. Grabbing his saddle as his strength was waning, he was able to saddle his horse one-handed. Trying to grab the apple of his saddle to swing up, Ed fell. Lying flat on his back was the last thing he remembered. It was now light in the livery. He had passed out, losing his chance to escape. His mouth was dry. His shoulder was on fire. He could feel his shirt crusted over with blood, with still fresh blood trickling down his neck and armpit. Ed's horse was still saddled and shied away from him and the smell of blood. There was no way he could leave the fort right now during the day, but he was sitting duck here in the livery. He lost his gun last night in getting away. Where was his knife? There were so many soldiers all of a sudden last night, he had panicked.

"You look pretty stoved up. They're looking for you," John said, staring down at Ed while leaning on a shovel.

"I had a little problem last night." Ed was judging his situation.

"I'd stay right where you're at until dark if I was you."

"I need water and to take care of this wound. What's your name?"

"John, I'll see what I can do about the wound. I can get you some water."

"Thanks," Ed went back to sleep.

"Hey, hey…hey, I got you some things," John said, shaking Ed's boot to wake him.

"What…oh, thanks," drinking water from the offered canteen.

"I brought you a clean shirt. I also brought some bandages. Figure we need to get that wound cleaned and bandaged."

"You know what happened, and you are a soldier. You could easily turn me in, and I could do nothing about it. Why are you helping me?" Ed questioning motive.

"I didn't like that girl and her filthy Indian grandparents. Her flaunting her money around here like she is better than everyone else. Hell, I figured you were doing a service getting rid of them."

"I had pard with me. Do you know what happened to him? Did he get away?"

"You don't know then? …He's dead. That Josie girl killed him with her Bowie."

"We been riding together for better than seven years…we have ridden the river together," Ed grimly.

"They planted him on boot hill this morning."

John bandaged Ed up and kept him concealed until nightfall. Ed had lost a site of blood and felt as weak as a kitten. Weak or not, that night Ed headed for Denver. He planned to come back to Fort Laramie. He wasn't done with that girl…Josie. He made a valuable friend in that John fellow back at Fort Laramie. John hated that girl too and would be useful later when he came back. He needed to go whole up for a while and lick his wound. Then, Ed needed to make some money. The only way he was willing to…with the least amount of effort possible. Other people could work; Ed was an artist on the dark fringe of the law. Unfortunately, he lost his partner, a new one could be acquired.

It was the stupid man that went to toil every day at a job. He had tried trapping up in Canada, punched a few cows in Texas…for what? The work was lonely and hard. It was too cold in Canada, too hot in Texas. Where were the saloons? Action? Women? The worse thing he ever tried to do was be a gambler. Those four-flushers have some skills. He could never get the sly swiftness of the card hand exchange completely downright. He had the art of card manipulation down then. He got into a poker game in New Orleans. Those people are not tinhorn gamblers. They are professionals. Played three hands, then realizing their game was staged to line their pockets, he excused himself to the necessary, leaving his money on the table. Ed was warned that if he got indebted to these people he was gambling with, they would kill him. He had been arrogant and thought his game was superior.

Dodging down a narrow-ally-ways, he made it back to where his horse was stabled. Needing money led to an act of desperation. The liveryman was an old man sleeping tipped back in his chair. The memory is so vivid the air thick with the humid scent of manure and horses, the old man was snoring peacefully. On cat-like feet walking up to him, he still didn't wake. The blade was

quick across his throat; he only woke and choked for a moment, not knowing what had happened. Then Ed drug his body into the back room, his living-quarters, and searched for money. There was some, as much as was left on the table. He killed three more people in the livery that night with his knife. He stacked the bodies in the back room and put fresh hay over the blood. Then all he had to do was wait in the shadows for the suitable victim to come his way. Later he locked the backroom door acquiring a tidy sum and a set of pistols and left New Orleans.

The bad thing about living this way is you're always on the move. Never just get to relax. It is a bad policy to be around when there is any questioning about murders, robberies, horse thefts…especially when you're guilty. You can stay around longer if there is a good place for the bodies, like a swift-moving river. Abandon mine shafts or dry wells are even better because there is no risk of the body washing up somewhere. A person has to pick their victim carefully. It would be a shame to waste your time. They have to have money or valuables that can be identified. They need to be vulnerable, drunk, weak, maybe a woman. It is absolutely essential to have a plan to dispose of the body first. Kill your victim at your disposal site. It would be awful to have to carry a body halfway across St. Louis and risk getting caught because of poor planning. When he and Col met up, it worked out great because they could work as a team. Col would watch assayers' offices or banks or saloons. Then without ever being seen, he could detain the person and take care of business. He and Col were a little bit richer. The two-person method allowed him to stay places longer and pick better marks.

***

The morning came quickly to Josie's camp. It had been late when she rolled it her sogun. Grandmother woke before her this morning starting the coffee. Grandfather was awake, sitting next to the fire smiling at Josie while drinking his cup of coffee. Why was she so tired? Josie had better hurry and wake up and take care of the stock. Jumping out of bed, she realized that her head was a little light. Her arm was searing, burning pain and worse when moved. Shaking her head to clear it of the dizziness, Grandmother handed her a cup of steaming hot coffee. Josie smiled at the grandparents, grateful they were part

of her life. Today her little family was starting home, where ever that may be.

"Thank you for the coffee, Grandmother. I am sorry I slept so late this morning."

"My little one, you are a wounded warrior. When you lose blood, you will be weak and tired. It is not spoken of to feel weak and tired. It is expected little one."

"It is only a small injury. It is of no importance. I will be fine, Grandmother."

"Granddaughter, you are a good warrior. I am proud of you. You fought well last night. You showed no fear."

"What of both of you last night? You both knew exactly how to jump in and help."

"Granddaughter, we are old and have fought all our lives in many battles. You are young and have proven yourself in battle," Grandfather smiling.

"Thank you, Grandfather...I just done what had to be done. I need to milk the cows now and get us loaded for the day," Josie said while looking at the ground, simultaneously sitting her cup down, feeling awkward about the compliment.

Josie was just finishing milking the Jerseys when behind her she heard footsteps. Immediately ready for action to fight Ed. Turning around quickly, there stood George and Paul, both smiling at her.

"We brought our cups. Thought we could bother you for a cup of coffee," George all smiles.

"You startled me. Grandmother has coffee on. I need to load the pack train, then I'll be over to have another cup of coffee before we go."

"We can help you load Miss Josie. We need to stow our gear in the wagon anyway. The colonel said the two scouts will be over to the camp before long."

"You been loading this pack train all by yourself all the way over the trail?" Paul asked, lifting a pack-saddle onto one of the Jennies.

"Yep, it was hard at first. Then you develop a pattern, and it isn't as difficult. Sometimes tying down the chicken cages can be a chore. Those little critters will peck you right through their cages," lifting a pack-saddle into place on one of the Jerseys.

The train was finished being loaded in no time, with three people doing the job. They walked over to the fire where Grandfather and Grandmother were visiting. The smell of the coffee and fire was homey.

"Grandmother, is there any coffee left for George and Paul?"

"I just made some more coffee; come and sit down," Grandmother had a big, partially toothy smile.

"My Granddaughter is a great warrior. She did battle last night. Would you like to hear of her great victory?" Grandfather said, dark eyes shining with pride. All of the creases of his age face moved in alignment with his huge grin. Josie, at this moment, wanted to hide. He then preceded to tell the story of last night's events. Grandfather added something Josie was not sure of, though.

"Grandfather, I am not sure my bullet struck the other man."

"I am. I saw the bullet hit Ed in the upper chest. Then look there is drops of blood that go away from camp," he continues his story, "Even though she had been shot, she does not cry. She has the heart of a great brave," he recounts the story with all the skill befitting a sage storyteller of his age.

"Miss Josie, you got shot last night?" George's eyebrows raised in concern, his voice elevated slightly.

"It is nothing really. I was shot through the arm. I'm fine," Josie said, a little sharper than she meant to.

Josie was saved from any further conversation by two men in buckskin. One of the men was awfully familiar…Rocky Pete. The other was at least six feet tall with blonde hair and piercing blue eyes. Neither had seen a razor in months from the look of it, and their hair was overgrown. She didn't care. Rocky Pete was a good guy, and if this guy was with Pete, he had to be good also.

"Hello, in the camp. Do you have any more coffee for a couple thirsty men?" the man beside Pete said.

"Rocky Pete and any friend of his is welcome to coffee," Josie said back.

"My name is Johansson people call me 'Handy.' I see you know Pete. The colonel set us to guide this group up to the Tormey Ranch up on the North Laramie River. Any of you ever been over there?" He was coolly studying this group composed of a

girl and two ancient Indians with two greenhorn Army kids riding along.

Josie excused herself to finish a piece of last-minute business while everyone got acquainted, finished their coffee, and double-checked the loads on the wagons. Josie knew there was a piece of business that needed attention, and it could not wait until the next time she was here. With a purposeful stride, she walked outside the confines of the fort to boot hill and found her father's marker. Stopping, Josie placed a finger over the rough wood then gently brushed the top edge of the plaque with her finger. As she did this, all sound seemed to fade out…time was at a stand-still. The prairie wind was whipping her skirt around her legs; she stood frozen. Head hung, braids falling forward, steaming hot tears slid off her cheeks, falling to her father's grave. Hiccupping sobs fell from her that she didn't try to repress. As the torrent of tears came to an end, Josie made a brief statement, "Pa, Ma is gone. I'll make the ranch work. I love you." Josie stood there smelling the sagebrush and looking at the grass, remembering what a hard-working, brilliant, lovable man he was. She closed her eyes and remembered what a remarkable woman her mother was. Her parents were physically gone, but they still lived on in what they taught her.

"I, Josie Tormey, will live on…I will continue to embrace the gifts my parents gave me, but my journey continues onward," Josie's voice rang out to the open prairie beside her father's grave while her eyes were on the distant mountains.

Josie's Journey: The Ranch

Coming Soon

Josie has successfully made it across the country at the cusp of the Civil War. She now has to build a life out in the frontier during the turbulence of two other wars, prejudice, and country expansion. If that wasn't enough for her to deal with, there is still some unsettled business…

Made in the USA
Middletown, DE
15 May 2022

65788123R00142